DOLLY

The Journey

Jan Dixon

Knockland Press

With love to - Caitlin, David, William, Victoria, Ruth and Kevin.

REVISED EDITION 2024

Dolly – The Journey
a
Biography

I am grateful to the following people who have given me information, advice and help in the preparation of Dolly – The Journey.

John Gelder whose research work in Kalimpong provided valuable early background information on Dolly.

The Rev Dr John Webster, Isle of Arran, on Dolly's early life and Dr Graham's Homes.

Alex Young for encouragement, meticulous research online, in newspapers and in the National Library Edinburgh and giving me the confidence to edit, edit and re-edit.

Alan Young for illustrations and answering all my questions on computer layouts and a million other things.

The late Mrs Virginia Smalley for trusting me with Dolly's scrap book, letters and photos.

The Prologue
Christchurch - South Island, New Zealand
25th October 1954

The faded blue floral curtains fluttered with the sweep of the cooler fan. The patient in the end bed lay still. Her arms had ceased flaying. Her breathing had grown quieter, and with each faint breath Virginia strained against the general buzz in the ward and hum of the fan to hear if there was any breath at all. At three o'clock in the afternoon a final gasp came. Twenty-one-year-old Virginia was now alone.
With a deep sigh she smoothed her green checked cotton skirt, and running her hand through her dark hair, tilted her head back and gazed unseeing at the white ceiling, her hand lingering on her tightening throat. Slowly dropping her head forward, her hand sliding down the front of her soft cream cotton blouse, and with both hands resting on her lap, her fingers entwined, her knuckles white, she took a deep breath, held it for a moment, an eternity, before letting it go.

The staff nurse pulled back the floral curtain a fraction, looked round glancing at Virginia, then at the patient, realising that Dolly's time on earth was over. Placing a comforting hand on Virginia's shoulder, and saying she was sorry, asked if she would like a cup of tea. Accepting the offer, Virginia stood and quietly pulled back the green metal chair. Bending down she picked up her brown handbag then, tentatively lent over lightly kissing her mother on the forehead, before following the staff nurse to the sister's office. Leaving the now quieter murmur of the ward, and two young nurses to attend to Dolly's lifeless body.

Virginia savoured the welcome warmth of the tea, served in a small rosebud patterned cup, kept for such occasions, she imagined. No-one spoke as she sipped the tea, and there was a sense of peace in the office of an otherwise busy, though now subdued, ward.

Eventually, with practicalities over, Virginia thanked the sister and staff nurse for their kindness and understanding, then made her way along the long corridor, never glancing round.

In the main hallway leading to the hospital's riverside access, as she approached the glass entrance, Virginia was suddenly aware of quickening footsteps behind her, saw and slowly recognised her older brother reflected in the glass door. She stopped, and he came round in front of her staring into her pale, tired face. 'She's gone Sid, you're too late,' Virginia told him.

Sid opened the door, and they descended the broad stone steps, leading to the walkway by the bank of the river Avon, no words passing between them. They crossed the little wooden bridge. Still with nothing further being said, Virginia stretched out her hand gently touching her brother's arm. She walked on towards Hagley Park exit, her eyes dry, her heart racing, leaving Sid standing alone watching her. His little sister was now a young woman and it seemed, like him, alone.

Turning right along Cambridge Terrace, passing Montreal Street to join Oxford Terrace to the junction of Hereford Street and into Cathedral Square. Finding an empty bench Virginia sat, staring blindly at the late afternoon's shoppers purposely heading in all directions. A sense of isolation encircled her. She slowly gathered herself together and headed for the bus stop and home. Fortunately, she did not have long to wait for the bus to Sydenham, the suburb of Christchurch where she and her mother Dolly had lived, above the baker's shop. So much to arrange and to attend to, that her thoughts took her far from the passing scene. She should have spoken kinder to Sid; it wasn't like her. The surprise at seeing him after sixteen years, and just following their mother's death, was too much too late.

Sid stood for a moment watching his sister, before turning round and slowly walking back through the pale, spring, October sunlight, to where he had left his bike padlocked against the fence by the riverside.

JANDIXON

Sadly, Virginia had not glanced round.

CHAPTER 1

Darjeeling to Calcutta, India
April 1897

The handsome red roofed, two storied Eden Sanatorium, or Eden Hospital opened in April; 1883, standing on a separate spur beyond the Cart Road in Darjeeling, was quiet and peaceful basking in the warm noonday sun. Sir Ashley Eden, a kind and highly esteemed diplomat of British India was responsible for building the sanatorium, exclusively built for the Europeans and Anglo Indians. Inside, in the cool stillness, five-year-old Dolly sat on her father's knee sobbing softly against his shoulder, as they sat by her mother's bedside watching, powerlessly, as Margaret slipped slowly from them. Lifting Dolly from her father's comforting embrace, Sister Sybil took Dolly's hand and led her from the room to allow Frederick to say his last goodbyes to his beloved young wife. He was due back in Calcutta soon, before heading north again to the Assam plantation, and the thought foremost in his mind was, who was going to look after his daughter. Irrespective of wealth, or lack of it, colour or creed, consumption spared no-one. Frederick started the arrangements for the funeral before collecting Dolly and thanking Sister Sybil, before returning to the Alice Villa Hotel where they had been staying during Margaret's last days.

Next morning the little funeral party gathered in the grounds of Darjeeling's St Andrew's Church. The old Christian graveyard, a little piece of England, high above the sweltering plains and plateaux of this vast land, where the first settlers, missionaries, administrators and founder of British Darjeeling, Dr Archibald

Campbell were buried. He was a British resident in Nepal, given charge of administration and responsible for the initial development of Darjeeling. The building of roads, maintaining law and order, and abolishing bonded slavery. Eventually becoming a peaceful hill station, growing and flourishing as communication improved, and known as the *Queen of Hills*. It would be Margaret's resting place too, alongside her recently deceased mother, who had also succumbed to consumption. Dolly held on tightly to her father's hand as they followed the coffin. The minister's words, read from the Common Prayer Book, floated high into the clear air merging with the many multi-coloured prayer flags fluttering in the morning breeze in the foothills of the Himalayas. Margaret was laid to rest far from her Buckinghamshire home with only her husband, daughter, Sister Sybil and the minister present.

Two days later Dolly watched the scenery unfold as she and Frederick set out on the 50-mile journey to Siliguri on the narrow-gauge railway, opened some twenty years earlier by the Darjeeling Himalayan Railway Company. Known as the Toy Train, the line followed the contours of the Hill Cart Road, skirting the fronts of shops and markets stalls, with occasional stops allowing passengers to buy refreshments. The train's horn almost without pause, warned people of its approach adding to the cacophony of noise which is India. The magnificent snow-capped Himalayan panorama revealed itself, and Dolly gazed in wonder, her eyes shining. It would be three years and in different circumstances till she would look out on this wondrous scene again. Frederick sat quietly, reflecting. This vast rich continent which gave so much, yet took what you held most dear. Soon the little family arrived at Siliguri surrounded by teagardens, changing trains for the 360-mile journey to the spread of India's then capital, Calcutta, along the eastern bank of the Hooghly River. Frederick and Margaret had lived in Calcutta since arriving from England six years earlier. Dolly, an only child, had been born in the capital spending five happy years there with her mother, growing up in a comfortable house in the suburbs, surrounded by large gardens and with servants to take care of their every need.

Noisily the huge beast of a train came to a shuddering halt at Sealdah Station, set up in 1869 and named after a village of jackals. The train sounded seemingly as tired as the myriad of passengers who now scrambled from doors, windows, running boards and roofs to join the vibrant and creative blend of West Bengalis already milling about the busy station, attending to their daily errands. Frederick, holding on tightly to Dolly's warm little hand, hailed a hand-pulled rickshaw, a recognised symbol of Calcutta. Carefully loading their small travelling chest and then seating Dolly and himself cautiously, not to unbalance the rickshaw, they headed home, away from the bustling station, south towards the White Town, the predominantly British area, centred on Chowringhee and Dalhousie Square. Chowringhee, the most fashionable thoroughfare in Calcutta, equated to what Piccadilly was to London, Fifth Avenue to New York and the Champs Elysees to Paris. Amazing, considering over hundred years and more before, the area was a jungle where elephants were hunted and beyond were pools, bamboo-groves, swamps and water-logged paddy-fields, with straggling huts for fishermen, wood-cutters, weavers and farmers.

The stillness within the cream-coloured stone-built house which greeted Frederick and Dolly reflected the air of sadness the servants felt at the loss of their young memsahib. With bowed heads and praying hands the servants greeted Frederick. The ayah, Dolly's nursemaid, gently led her charge upstairs. She bathed her, change and dressed her in a fresh white cotton frock. Dolly, having eaten little was then taken to see her father before her long overdue nap. Frederick looked deeply into his young daughter's normally bright, but now sad, tired eyes. Taking her hands in his he gently told her that soon he would have to return to the tea plantation in Assam, but that his sister, her Aunt Dorothea, would be arriving from England to take her back to the family home in Buckinghamshire, where she would be living with her Uncle William, Aunt Mary and her three cousins, Henry, Victoria and young William.

Dolly fell into her father's arms frightened that she was losing him so soon after losing her kind and gentle mother. Holding her closely, Frederick patiently explained that Calcutta was not a place for a young girl to grow up in alone, even although she did have an ayah and servants to look after her. The house would be closed while he was away managing the plantation and although Dolly would grow up in England, as soon as possible, after her schooling was over, he would send for her and they could be together again.

Her maiden aunt, Dorothea, would be sailing out from England and would arrive within three weeks. In the meantime, preparations would go ahead for Dolly's voyage to England and her new home. Dolly had learned about England – a cool and pleasant land through her mother's bedtime stories. The Higgins family lived in the beautiful village of Hambleden. A village of red brick and flint cottages, surrounded by the lush green English countryside with a landmark 14th-century church, St Mary's. There was a watermill, Hambleden Mill and like Calcutta on the Hooghly River, the village too was situated by a river, the Thames. Yet somehow after the noisy, extraordinarily colourful assortment of life she had grown up with in Calcutta, England held no excitement for Dolly. Especially now her mother was no longer there and her father too would soon be away, back to Siliguri and on to the tea garden high in the Darjeeling Hills.

She shivered, this was too much for a young girl to take in, pulling herself from her father's gentle embrace she ran up to her room, collapsing on to her bed sobbing.

CHAPTER 2

Christchurch, New Zealand

25th October 1954

Sid slipped on his bicycle clips, undid the padlock on his bicycle which was against the fence and cycled along the riverside walkway towards the park. He decided to sit for a while amongst the last of the daffodils instead of heading back to his rooms. His work was over for the day; tomorrow he would hopefully finish his decorating job on this side of town. Maybe the family would recommend him, he would just have to wait and see. At least here in the park there was be some distractions with the chatter and giggling from the students from the nearby college wandering home through the gardens at the end of classes. A few dogs ran about barking and chasing sticks, enjoying the afternoon spring sunshine. 'Virginia must be about eighteen years old now, I wonder if she has a job, maybe a shop assistant or office job, perhaps', Sid speculated, as he gazed out over the recreation ground. 'I was surprised she recognised me after all this time'.

Sid arrived back in Christchurch in 1952 shortly after his father, Sidney Stewart, had died. Realising there was little work for him in Coal Creek, he decided to use the money from the sale of the lease of the farm to start a new life. He headed east hoping to find work in the city. He had helped his father on the farm since running away from the St Joseph's Boys Home in Christchurch many years before in 1938. His father never questioned why he had run away and young Sid never spoke about it. He seemed happy to be home and that was all that mattered.

Memories of the Home sent dreadful shudders through his body, and feelings of anxiety still haunted him. He closed his eyes trying to shake off the feelings of futility, which still seemed to follow him. The sound of two girls laughing nearby brought him back to the present. His older half-brother Doug, who also lived in Christchurch, and had been in touch with him recently, letting him know that their mother was ill in hospital with stomach cancer. Debating within himself whither to go and see Dolly, he decided he could not face her again after all these years, and being so ill, she would not be able to answer any of his long unanswered questions. Yet he had gone to the hospital, but too late. Having spoken with Doug briefly, Sid realised that he too had very little contact with their mother Dolly. He was however, pleased to learn that his brother was married and settled in Christchurch. Strange how life takes inexplicable turns.

Dolly had kept his young sister Virginia, but as Sid had seen today, she looked tired and weary, and now she too was alone. He had no way of finding her again unless he enquired at the hospital and he had a feeling they would not freely give out such information. 'Too late.' Virginia had said. Gathering his thoughts, Sid picked up his bike again and headed out of the park, making his way home. He decided to contact Doug to keep in touch, he had been so fond of his big brother all those years ago, but what could he tell him of his life? That he had run away too, back to his father, after leaving Dolly and Virginia in Christchurch all those years ago. The shame of his past had kept him withdrawn. So, Sid once again was alone with his memories,

CHAPTER 3
Calcutta
Late April 1897

Calcutta, the great centrepiece of the British Raj was the greatest colonial city of the Orient, one of four great urban centres of India. The mighty Victorian buildings of the city shone in the spring sun light, somehow defying the heat as it gathered across the plains and plateaux. It would be late May into early June before the European population would head for the cool freshness of the hill stations, before the onset of the monsoon in late June. By this time Dolly would be on her way with Aunt Dorothea to her new home in England.

The noise, bustle, smells and colour surrounding the port at Calcutta filled Dolly with bewilderment and excitement. She held tightly onto her father's hand watching the ship ease in along the side of the quay. The passengers crowded, peering over the side as Dolly looked up, eyes straining in the bright sunlight to see if she could pick out the lady who was her aunt among the crowd on deck. The acrid smell of rotting garbage thrown from ships and left floating on the tide; the hovering flies and the taste of warm dust mingled in Dolly's mouth and head making her wish she was back in the relative cool shade of the family garden, but mostly back safe with her mother. Her eyes filled with tears. After what seemed ages, Dorothea approached them through a crush of people, muttering about getting out of this dreadful place and wishing she was back in England. An Indian carrier brought her luggage and soon luggage and passengers were balanced on two rickshaws heading away from the docks, taking them to

Chowringhee.

Later in the day Dorothea appeared in the drawing room, refreshed from sleep. Bathed and dressed now in a silk, rose taffeta evening dress, an ivory and emerald clip in her upswept auburn hair, Dorothea looked younger than her years. Her brother, Frederick, offered her a chilled refreshment which she accepted graciously, walking over to the veranda to gaze out into the garden now dappled pink in the evening light, the sounds of an Indian evening filling her head, how far away England seemed. 'It's so kind of you to chaperone young Dolly back to England,' Frederick said, also making his position clear, 'This is no place for a young girl to grow up, now that dear Margaret has passed away.' He felt his throat tighten. Losing Margaret was one thing, but now Dolly, he felt his life's purpose slowly slip from him. However, soon he would have to travel north again, back to Assam to check out the plantation. Good as the workers were, he needed to be there, the plantation owner and the business needed him.

CHAPTER 4

Christchurch, New Zealand
October 1954

The knock at the door came exactly at 10 o'clock the next morning. Virginia had slept fitfully, her mind filled with her mother's last moments, and seeing Sid again, however fleetingly, after all these years. How strange it had felt.

Dolly had been ill for several months now, rarely leaving her bed. The doctor called in from time to time and left some medicine. Eventually the pain was so great that Dolly had been moved to the General Hospital in Christchurch. By then it was too late. She was well cared for, clean and comfortable and Virginia managed to visit her most days on her way home from work at Ballantine's, the large department store, Christchurch's Harrods they called it. The staff in the ward let her in a few minutes before tea time and she came to appreciate these quiet times alone with Dolly, knowing that her mother was in safe hands and pain free at last.

Virginia spent most evenings on her return from the hospital preparing and eating her meal, washing or ironing and tidying the two roomed apartment they rented. The baker's shop below closed promptly in the late afternoon as the baker himself started very early in the morning and Virginia had grown accustomed to waking to the welcome smell of newly baked bread. Virginia enjoyed looking at and rearranging the few pieces they had, inexpensive little ornaments Dolly had gathered over the years, a few mementos of other times and other places.

Dolly and Virginia had mostly kept themselves to themselves.

Now she missed the quiet evenings they shared, reading or listening to music on the radio, when Dolly would cast her mind back to one house she remembered. A large cream coloured house with large green exotic gardens and where the sun always seemed to shine. Then realising Virginia had stopped reading and was listening, Dolly would lower her eyes and no more mention would be made of the house and anyway she would say, 'I think it must have been a dream'. They had moved a few times within the city, leaving in the late evening, avoiding the neighbour's curiosity. Alex Smith, her second husband, had abandoned them, a couple of years after they had married. Abusive to Dolly right from the start, as well as drinking and womanising. Dolly, alone again with Virginia, had earned extra money in the afternoons, as many women did during and after the war entertaining male clients, which allowed the rent to be paid and put food on the table. Many clients she had met through her work at the Carlton Hotel, having strict instructions always to leave before Virginia arrived home from school

One ornament or souvenir Virginia always handled with care was the little silver rattle, Dolly's precious reminder of her long-lost baby, Nancy, or so she said. Nancy whom Dolly sometimes called out for in her now morphine induced state. She had always made a point of keeping the little rattle polished and safely wrapped in its white, lace-edged dolly-bag and no matter the hurry, she never forgot to put it in her bag before leaving, particularly when the rent was overdue.

Too late now to ask about Nancy, Virginia had pondered, the knock at the door interrupting her thoughts, and although expecting the knock, she jumped. She glanced in the mirror, sad eyes looked back at her, she smoothed her thick dark hair, checked the buttons on her blouse, stopped with her hand on the handle, took a deep breath, then quickly opened the door to reveal standing on the landing Mr Bloomfield, the undertaker, soberly dressed and with briefcase in hand.

CHAPTER 5

Calcutta, India
April 1897

Dorothea had agreed to stay on in the house in Calcutta till Margaret's belongings were organized and the house ready to be closed, awaiting Frederick's return from the plantation. There was much to do sorting out Margaret's clothes, jewellery, letters and ornaments, most of which would go back with them to Buckinghamshire, to the Higgins family home. Margaret had been the only child of an army colonel, who had been killed several years before, her mother succumbing to consumption not long before Margaret. It fell therefore to Frederick's family to sort out her affairs.

Dolly gradually came to accept her Aunt being in the house, and taking charge now that her beloved father had left for Assam. The day he left seemed to Dolly to be as sad as the day her dear mother died. He left early in the morning just after breakfast, Dolly clung to him till her Aunt Dorothea gathered her from him, handing her sobbing to the ayah, who smoothed Dolly's thick dark pleated hair, wiped her wet little face, and coaxed a smile her father would remember. The servants running hither and thither, gathering boxes and pieces of baggage ready for the carrier to take them to the station. Promising Dolly he would write soon, Frederick thanked Dorothea and kissed Dolly goodbye, his heart filled with much sadness at leaving his little daughter behind, not knowing when he would see her again. Blinking away tears Frederick left, never glancing round.

Dorothea spent the rest of the day trying to comfort Dolly. Though she had no children of her own, she had nieces and nephews, so looking after Dolly came naturally to her. In this heat she tired easily and of course, none of her other charges had suffered such sadness at such a young age. With the help of the ayah, and after some light food and cool drinks, Dolly rested in the heat of the afternoon. Dorothea too lay down in the cool of her room, quietly planning her best moves for keeping Dolly amused, as well as continuing her task of sorting out her late sister in law's treasures and closing down several rooms in the house, leaving the main rooms and their bedrooms till last. The servants busied themselves following her instructions, moving quietly so as not to disturb the new memsahib.

Dolly lay quietly on her bed, under the muslin mosquito net, the cool, cream silk sheet pulled up to her chin, tears drying on her cheeks, her dark hair now spread out over the cream embroidered pillow slip, the way her mother had smoothed it at bedtime. Her little princess she had called her. Remembering this, Dolly's eyes filled with fresh tears and she sobbed soundlessly to herself, before sleep overcame her and she drifted off to the hills above Darjeeling.

Early the next morning Dorothea decided to take Dolly to visit the Calcutta Botanical Gardens, on the west bank of the Hoogly River. Early morning in winter or spring was the best time to see the gardens. Countless birds of many species made their home there. In winter, migratory birds flew south to the Calcutta Botanical Garden from the Himalayan foothills, China and Siberia to restock on their food supply. Interesting sounding names like the Blue Throated Flycatcher, Black-hooded Oriole, Tickell's Thrush and the Eurasian Woodcock. Dorothea recognised the Kingfishers, Warblers and Woodpeckers also found on the banks of the River Thames, near her home in Hambleden in Buckinghamshire.

The Botanical Garden was also the home of the world's largest banyan tree, some 137 years old, even surviving two cyclones in the 1860s. Its aerial roots drooping from above to create the effect of a small forest, a magical place for a young child, Dorothea thought, as they both set out escorted by two of the servants. It would take most of the day but such an adventure would surely help Dolly and allow her get to know her Aunt, who also planned a visit to the red bricked New Market on Lindsay Street, which had

opened to some fanfare on 1st January 1874. This colossal Gothic-style building with a clock tower, had replaced the old Fenwick's Bazaar. The giant shopping arcade was thrown open exclusively to the English residents. Beneath the clock tower, the market stalls displayed endless arrays of garments, books, kitchenware, and silver jewellery in little curio shops. The most colourful stalls were those displaying fruit, vegetable and flowers. The noises, sounds and smells of the market were varied and colourful. Dolly remembered her mother bringing her a beautiful silver rattle from the market which she loved, polishing it and playing with it.

CHAPTER 6

Christchurch, New Zealand

28th October 1954

The Ruru Lawn Cemetery, in Bromley, Christchurch, opened in 1941. The Canterbury Provincial Memorial is situated in the RuRu Cemetery and commemorates 33 New Zealand servicemen of the 1914-1918 War and 10 New Zealand airmen from the 1939-1945 War. The servicemen who were either buried elsewhere in New Zealand or buried at sea or whom the fortunes of war denied a known and honoured grave. The victims of the infamous 1947 Ballantine's fire are also buried here. The store, a local institution, was destroyed by one of the worst fires in New Zealand history.

On the afternoon of Tuesday 18th November fire engulfed the department store in Cashel Street, central Christchurch. Of the 41 people who died; 39 were employees and two were external auditors, trapped by the fire, and overcome by smoke. The store, had neither a fire alarm or an evacuation plan. Of the 680 people in the store at the time of the fire, 430 staff and 250 customers, the final death toll could have been much worse.

The small cortege stopped at the gates on Raymond Road, and the small group of mourners, slowly and sedately, walked the short distance behind the pall bearers carrying Dolly's coffin to its final resting place. Virginia, her head bowed, followed with sweet-scented lilies in her right hand, and, in her left, the embroidered white cotton bag with the little silver rattle. The sun shone but the spring air was keen, fresh snow had topped the Southern Alps overnight, leaving them sharply sculptured against a blue sky. Over fifty years before, the morning sun had outlined the Himalayan peaks against a blue sky, as Margaret was lowered into her grave at Darjeeling. The air too had been keen and fresh. Dolly had cried. Today Virginia dried her eyes with her white lace-edged handkerchief, before placing the silver rattle on the coffin, to stay with Dolly forever.

A few of Virginia's friends from work and one or two neighbours shuffled their feet to keep warm, as the minister read the *Lord's My Shepherd*, said a prayer and committed the body. He then came forward and shook Virginia's, now cold hand, she thanked him and thanked the few who had gathered to say goodbye, before making her way back to the bus stop and home.

The next day Sid visited the cemetery, having enquired at the hospital as to where the funeral and burial would be. Not knowing, they put him in touch with the local undertaker, Bloomfields. Leaving his bike just inside the cemetery gate, Sid sought the help of a gardener, who pointed out the fresh grave mound with its floral tributes. He walked over to his mother's grave and stood, his head bowed, roughly wiping a few tears away. Turning he walked back towards the cemetery gate, not even acknowledging the gardener. Mounting his bike, he cycled off in the direction of town, angry with himself and puzzled too by the name *Doris Ethel Smith* inscribed on the little granite plaque and the dates *25th April 1900 – 25th October 1954*.

CHAPTER 7

The Shillong Earthquake, India
12th June 1897

Rolling hills, tall pine trees and chilly nights, gave this North Eastern Hill area of India a feeling of Scotland. Built on a one-thousand-year-old site in 1874, Shillong became Assam's capital. The area was a region of great scenic beauty - lush undulating hills, fertile valleys and vast forests - now transformed into beautiful tea gardens along the Brahmaputra and Barak River valleys, growing the best-loved black Assam tea. In 1839, the Assam Tea Company, formed in England, took over the tea plantations from the East India Company, which had developed the tea trade, previously monopolised by China. By 1860, a million pounds in weight of tea was being grown.

In Assam, day breaks before five o'clock in the morning and ends by five o'clock in the evening, and this was known as *Chai Bagan Time*. Frederick enjoyed his early morning walks through the greens of tea. Far from the madness and heat of Calcutta, it was a mild, cooling experience, the city could not offer. Here, now, he had time to reflect upon his beloved Margaret and give thought to his pretty little daughter Dolly, still living in Calcutta with his older sister Dorothea. He would go into Shillong in the afternoon and send a cable to Dolly from the telegraph office, letting her know he was on his way. Someday he would tell her about this land of Meghalaya – The abode above the clouds - and the exquisite butterflies and countless insects which flew or hovered over the meandering rivers, with their waterfalls and sparkling streams. The area was a picture book of natural wonder, for child and adult alike. Frederick rode into town on the Saturday afternoon feeling more contented than he had since Margaret's death, knowing Dolly was safe, and would be well looked after by his family in England, till she was old enough to return to India and be with him once again. The journey into town was strangely quiet, no singing birds, no barking dogs, and an uneasy quietness filled the humid air. Even his horse seemed uneasy in the eerie stillness.

The Great Shillong earthquake struck at 5.11pm, affecting an area the size of England. Masonry buildings, like the church, became a heap of stones in less than a minute, and the centre of Shillong vanished - buildings, people, and animals. The water burst from surrounding lakes leaving them dry in seconds. The magnitude of the earthquake was such, that it raised the northern edge of the Shillong Plateau; affecting the whole of Assam. Even several masonry buildings as far away as Calcutta were affected. 1,542 were killed, the town was razed to the ground and the surrounding hillsides with their tea gardens were ripped apart. The quake lasted for several minutes, till the noise quelled and all was still. As the dust settled, surviving dogs began a chorus of excited barking, and birds took up a riot of singing which continued well into the night.

Dolly, unknowingly, had become an orphan, her life changing dramatically.

CHAPTER 8

Christchurch, New Zealand
Late October 1954

Sid's two roomed apartment was above a little newsagent's shop, which also sold bread, milk, fresh fruit and vegetables. Sid liked his home and kept it smart and clean. He had taken to the painting and decorating job, which he had seen advertised in the newsagent's window, and had shown aptitude for the job. He was always on time, pleasant and helpful to customers, and minded his own business. Sid got on with the job and bothered no-one. Today had brought back many memories and although he had half promised to join workmate Ron for an evening pint, he decided instead to have a bottle of beer at home by himself. Some tea and a cheese and ham sandwich would suffice. It was an evening for memories, not company.

The snow on the Southern tops had cooled the air, and there was quite a chill by the time Sid reached home. Manoeuvring his bike into a space at the back of the yard he climbed the stairs, his key, for once, turning in the lock first time. Sid quickly opened the door, then closing it behind him, lent on it for a moment before hanging his warm tweed jacket up on its peg in the narrow hallway. Wandering into the kitchen he filled the kettle, putting it on to the electric ring to boil, before switching on one bar of the electric heater. He made himself a cheese and ham sandwich before sitting down in the old fireside chair, he rubbed his chilled hands together as he waited on the kettle boiling. With the piping hot mug of tea and sandwich, he returned to his chair. The warm sweet tea took his mind back to the years when he and older brother Doug were together on the farm at Coal Creek on the West Coast.

The eight-acre farm lay on the south bank of the Grey River north east of Greymouth, the Paparoa Range to the east and north, and the Southern Alps to the south and east. The meagre wooden farm buildings, a small farm house, a cowshed and a stable with a couple of horse-drawn wagons. Sid's father, Sydney Stewart, had taken on a £150 renewable lease in 1904 when he was 30 years old, working the farm with the help of itinerant labourers over the years. His first wife Catherine Rose had died in childbirth, their baby daughter Virginia Rose dying a few days later. Sid's father had been 52 years old when in September 1926 he married a striking, dark haired 35-year-old woman who had a young 5-year-old son Douglas, and called herself *Doreen Ethel Higgins* and put *born in Edinburgh* on their marriage certificate. Nancy was born nine months later, and young Sid was born in 1928 after the fire.

He had been six years old when his fourteen-year-old brother Doug ran away, planning to go to Nelson some 238 miles away. His step father had blamed Doug for the fire and the subsequent tragic death of baby Nancy. Young Sid never asked his mother or father about Nancy, but often heard Doug crying at night in their little attic room, and when he asked Doug what was wrong, he mumbled about him being blamed for what happened to Nancy. Sid always missed his brother, but he now had a two-year-old little sister Virginia, the year was 1935.

With the hot sweet tea and satisfying sandwich inside him, followed by a couple of beers, and the bit of warmth from the heater, sleep soon overcame Sid. He nodded off, with images of the West Coast flats flitting in and out of his mind.

CHAPTER 9

Calcutta, India
May 1897

News of the Assam earthquake was soon known across India. It was, however, many days before news of Frederick's disappearance, and presumed death, reached his sister in Calcutta, who had been waiting anxiously for news, frightened to breathe a word of her fears to young Dolly. With Frederick's death finally confirmed, Dorothea cabled her brother William in Hambleden, England, asking what was to be done now, regarding Dolly. Frederick's estate would need to be wound up. The house in Calcutta, and the small house on the plantation in Assam, although there was little, if any, of it left, and any monies would eventually be transferred to the family in Hambleden. Being the male heir, William would now have charge of the estate, and young Dolly.

Unquestionably William was needed in India to attend to all the business and paperwork. Dorothea would continue her care of Dolly till they decided what was best to do with her. William was not convinced taking her back to England was what he really wanted; India was, after all, her home, where she had been born. Within the fortnight William had his £55 first class ticket, to join the 1,127 others on the twelve-day sail from London's Tilbury Dock to Bombay, aboard the *SS Katoria*.

Arriving in India at the height of the monsoon season was certainly not to his liking.
With temperatures of around 90F and rainfall of 25" in Bombay,

the continued journey across India to Calcutta by train was arduous and hazardous, and this certainly did not help William's disposition. In Calcutta the temperatures were even higher. Dorothea was wishing she too was far from the rain and heat of the city. Most English people had moved to the hill stations weeks before. Siliguri, located on the banks of the Mahananda River, being the closest hill station to Calcutta, where temperatures hovered around 66F, a more bearable, comfortable heat.

Having spent over three weeks putting the finishing touches to the tidying and clearing of Margaret's belongings and clothes, closing down the bedrooms and other unused rooms, Dorothea was tired. Although a few of the staff had stayed on to help look after her and Dolly, she was pleased William would soon be with them. She also learned from William's cable that the plans for Dolly had changed, and on a couple of occasions, while Dolly slept in the afternoon, Dorothea had called on St Mary's House of Charity, in Calcutta's Sooterkin's Lane, and spoken to Dr John Comely, the Honorary Treasurer, and his wife Mrs Alice Comely, the Secretary and lady manager of the 'Home'.

Founded in 1888 as a charity to support the Christian poor of Calcutta, it relied on subscriptions and donations of money and furniture. The condition of the poor had awakened British public sympathy with the Committee appealing for such help as they could afford. St Mary's building had suffered damage during the Assam earthquake, especially the two upper floors, so with this in mind William Higgins felt that donating to the Home would be a way to approach them as a future sanctuary for Dolly. A reasonable monetary donation and the furniture from Frederick's house, would be acceptable. Now with a clear conscience he and Dorothea could leave for England and home, far from this land of intense heat, carved temples and gleaming marble palaces, thronging multitudes and grinding poverty.

CHAPTER 10

St Mary's Homes for Anglo-Indian Ladies
Calcutta, India

In the early 18th century the Carnatic region of south east India, between the Coromandel coast and the Eastern Ghats, saw the first 'Female Asylums', where Christian missionaries took in female babies to save them from infanticide. They were brought up in the Christian faith, some later finding husbands in the British Army. A second generation of illegitimate children, fathered by British soldiers, were also taken in to these asylums to be educated.

After the 1745 Jacobite Rebellion in Britain, many surviving Scottish soldiers, and those who had not been executed, were transported to the Carnatic. One can only guess at the number of Indo-Scottish children born in, and out of wedlock, who would need the protection of these missionaries.

Female asylums flourished in garrison towns where the regiments were posted, as a place of refuge, not only for the young female children, but for the concubines, active or abandoned. These Asylums were nothing but Japanese style 'comfort stations' for British soldiers to use the women as the whim took them. All the while the Madras Archdeaconry sent priests on regular tours to these asylums to baptise or bury children only, as most of the women were non-Christian.

The Sanctuaries that once dotted British India developed into the first Christian schools as the conscience of the British East India

Company Service, and the British Army in particular, began to take effect, and so it was into this system that William Higgins had decided to place Dolly.

CHAPTER 11

Christchurch, New Zealand
October 1954

It was a tired Virginia who arrived back at her flat in Sydenham to find the front door now ajar, knowing she had locked it when leaving for her mother's funeral, that morning. Only she and her mother had a key, and as Dolly had been bedridden and hospitalised, Virginia knew the spare key would be in her mother's bedside drawer. On her way to check the drawer by the bed recess in the living room, she hung her coat and shoulder bag up on a peg in the passageway. She stopped and listened, no noise, the flat felt empty. On entering the small living room, a dark figure loomed between her and the light from the window. Virginia gasped, heart pounding, as she turned to run. The man lunged, catching her by the arm, shoving her roughly out of the room and back against the entrance wall. It was Dolly's estranged husband, Virginia's step father, Alex Smith. He had taken nothing to do with them, despite living in rented rooms nearby, and had never visited Dolly throughout her illness. Virginia had seen him at the bus stop, and although he never acknowledged her, one morning she plucked up courage to tell him about Dolly's illness. He had merely grunted. Now here he was in their sparsely furnished flat, demanding her key, and telling her to waste no time in gathering her belongings as she no longer lived here. It was now his flat and she could fend for herself.

Stumbling and weeping, Virginia gathered what clothing she could from behind her bedroom door, shoving them into a well-worn suitcase from under her bed. Some makeup, a hairbrush, comb and a small trinket box, she hurriedly put into an old shopping bag which she had tripped over in the hurry to escape Smith's threats and mutterings. Snatching the shopping bag and shoulder bag from her, Smith threw both out onto the landing, pushing a struggling Virginia and her suitcase, out after them. The door slammed shut behind her. Where could she go now, who could she contact. Fear filled her as she trembled and gasped for breath. The thud of the bags on the landing floor brought the memory of the first sod hitting the coffin lid only hours before. Each had a finality. Taking a deep breath, straightening herself, and sorting her coat, picking up her case and bags she slowly and carefully made her way down stairs and out into the street. She didn't look back.

Smith watched her from the window till she turned the corner. He had only been married to Dolly for a few years, before he left. A few years in which he had verbally and often physically abused her, though not in his eyes. As Virginia was not his daughter, he had no obligation to support her. Looking round, Smith thought that the flat though sparsely furnished, was cheaper than his, so the idea of moving was tempting. In the morning, he would contact the factor. Smith put his key in the lock, and closed the door behind him.

Virginia took a bus across the city to her friend Jean's house, knowing she would get a bed for a night or two. In the morning she would look for a place of her own before returning to work. Ballantine's had given her a few of days off for the funeral and to sort things out, but little had she thought that once again she would be homeless.

However, there was always hope.

CHAPTER 12

St Mary's Homes,
23 Marquis Street, Calcutta,
India

Mrs Alice Comely, the secretary of St Mary's Homes, was born in Lambeth, London, in August 1850 to Augusta Cleere and John St Clement Wooltorton from Norfolk, a Corrector of the Press, marrying Augusta in St Mary's, Lambeth, in May 1844. By the mid nineteenth century there were an estimated 300 proof readers or correctors of the press in the city - their headquarters adjoined the home of Dr Samuel Johnston - poet, satirist, and lexicographer - at 17 Gough Square, London. The 'correctors' were poorly paid, only two earning more than £2 per week working a 45–60 hour week.

So it was that the Wooltortons decided to migrate to India in 1855 with three of their young children. On the voyage their ship was wrecked off the coast of Zanzibar. All were saved. On arriving in India, they settled first in Bombay, before moving to Calcutta, where their father died in August 1862 and was buried in the Episcopalian Burial Ground. In May 1870 Alice married John Muspratt Comely M.R.C.S. who had trained at Guy's Hospital, London, a son of surgeon John Comely, of St Johns, Calcutta. Alice and John lived many years at 12 Chowringhee Road, in the city, with their six children. Each being sent back to England to be educated, looked after there by a widowed aunt, a widowed friend, a domestic nurse and a housemaid. After the young Comleys education was complete, they returned to India where they married and settled down.

The couple were of a charitable disposition and many of Calcutta's poor had reason to remember their many good deeds, all done unostentatiously. John had in a quiet and unobtrusive way improved the sanitary conditions of the city, making it a healthier place. At his death in December 1911, aged 74 years, he was one of Calcutta's oldest residents and certainly its oldest medical practitioner. Well known for her charity work amongst the poor, Mrs Comely had founded St Mary's Home for the Poor, an institution providing shelter and care for Calcutta's many poor, widowed, and abandoned women, and children, many orphaned as Dolly now was. In January 1910, she was awarded the *Kaisar-i-Hind medal* - Emperor of India medal in Hindi for first class public service. Alice herself died in 1919 aged 69 years at her home in London's Portman Square.

-oOo-

Leaving Dolly with her ayah, William and Dorothea made their way to St Mary's Home for their meeting with Alice Comley, to arrange Dolly's future care. Being a Caucasion orphan, she qualified for acceptance, but the final decision lay with the Committee of European Civilians of Settlement, the lady Directoresses of the Home. As an orphan with no means of support - William having taken Frederick's estate but not the responsibility of Dolly's future. With no last will and testament found stating Frederick's wishes, William was not legally bound to provide for her.

With the Shillong earthquake having swept away the plantation, Frederick's estate consisted only of the house in Calcutta. A tidy sum for William Higgins's none the less, without taking on the burden of Dolly. Having her back in England would be a constant reminder of India - so leaving Dolly in St Mary's allowed them to go home to continue their uncomplicated lives, a little more comfortably, in Buckinghamshire.

An agreement was reached with Alice Comely. The contents of

Frederick's house and 150 Rupees being accepted. Satisfied with this arrangement William and Dorothea returned to Chowringhee Road delighted with the outcome of their visit.

Dolly was now officially an orphan and her future someone else's responsibility .

CHAPTER 13

St Mary's Homes,
Calcutta, India
June 1897

Busy watching the birds wash and preen in the monsoon puddles, Dolly hadn't seen Dorothea send the ayah upstairs as she and William entered the house. On hearing their voices, she ran excitedly from the sitting room into the large entrance hall to welcome her aunt and uncle. At the same moment the ayah came from upstairs carrying a large portmanteau filled with Dolly's clothes. Dismissed, she disappeared to the rear of the house, weeping. Telling her of the new arrangements, Dolly struggled as her aunt put her blue Sunday cape around her shoulders. Dorothea assured her that she would be well looked after in her new home, and she would still be in Calcutta. Asking if her father was waiting there for her, her hopes were dashed by William's negative reply. Dolly started to cry, louder and louder, her small body trembling. Loosening herself from her aunt's hold, she ran up the wide staircase to her bedroom, pushing the door open ran around in her search for the silver rattle her mother had given her. Finding it partially hidden by the frill of the pale pink damask curtain, Dolly picked it up and held it close. Then putting it in its little white lace trimmed dolly-bag she hid it in her cape pocket. Still sobbing, she made her way down stairs to face her future, never lifting her eyes and never looking at her aunt or uncle.

The carrier lifted the large coloured bag off the front step, and William, Dorothea and Dolly followed him to the rickshaw for their journey to St Mary's, no one spoke. Dolly would never forget

William and Dorothea's return that fateful afternoon. As the rickshaw moved off, she never looked back at her former home.

Alice Comely took young Dolly in to her care, and for the next three years Dolly was looked after by the governesses and nurses of St Mary's, mainly the charitable ladies of Calcutta. It was in these surroundings that Dolly learnt to read, write and count. There was always company in the Home, with little time to be sad. Dolly however, still sorely missed her mother and father, frequently puzzling why her aunt and uncle had sent her away and why her father had not come for her. Dolly thrived in St Mary's, and at the turn of the century, Alice Comley decided it would be best for Dolly and one of the other girls, Dolly's friend, Maggie Leslie, to move from Calcutta to the newly opened St Andrew's Colonial Homes in Kalimpong, nestling in the foothills of the Himalayas. It was run by her friend Dr John Anderson Graham of Edinburgh, a young Scottish missionary who in 1903, had also been awarded the Kaiser-i-Hind medal, and his wife Katherine.

CHAPTER 14
Darjeeling, India
1900

In the spring of 1900 Dolly and Maggie caught colds which developed into chest infections, so Dr Comley advised they be sent north to the Eden Sanatorium in Darjeeling for recuperation.

The girls had become good friends over the three years they had been in St Mary's. Maggie's father William Leslie, like Dolly's, was a tea planter in Assam, though her mother had been a native *wife* abandoned by William with the arrival of his wife from England, in 1897. William had been in Calcutta to meet his wife at the time of the earthquake, having earlier taken Maggie, to St Mary's, having previously arranged a substantial payment for her upkeep. As Dolly and Maggie's friendship grew Dolly had shared her silver rattle with Maggie, who had no keepsakes of her life with her mother in the tea gardens, just sadness and fading memories.

On Dr Comely's recommendation the St Mary's committee arranged for the girls to travel north to Darjeeling by train chaperoned by committee member, Miss Arbuthnot. The fresh hill air would do them the world of good. Alice Comely realised with the girls being in Darjeeling, they could continue on to the newly opened St Andrew's Homes, previously the Kalimpong Mission and into the care of Dr Graham rather than returning to Calcutta. Her husband agreed, and so the correspondence with Dr Graham began. Dolly's life would take another turn, this time under the watchful gaze of Mount Kanchenjunga.

-oOo-

Boarding the train at Calcutta, Dolly, Maggie and their chaperone had a long journey ahead of them to reach the quiet, Ghoom Junction in the Darjeeling Himalayan region of West Bengal. It took longer than usual having many stops and engine trouble as it climbed to a height of over 7,000 feet, the highest railway station in India, above the cooler but dusty sprawling townships of Jalpaiguri and Siliguri. Transferring to the Darjeeling Himalayan Railway, *The Toy Train* at Siliguri, to take them on through luscious forests and recently replanted tea gardens to Darjeeling.

Dolly had last been on this line with her father a few days after her mother's funeral, as they returned home to Calcutta. How long ago that now seemed, so much having happened in her young life, so much having changed. She remembered the spectacular panorama as the morning mists cleared, the snow-capped peaks seemingly suspended in the air above Darjeeling, it all became too much for Dolly and she started to cry, much to Miss Arbuthnot's concern. Her young charge cried softly as she held her trying to reassure her all would be well. Soon they would reach the safety of the sanatorium where they could rest and get their strength back. Miss Arbuthnot knew nothing of Dolly's previous experience on this journey. Dolly had kept the memories to herself, as at her age she had neither the words to explain or the courage to tell.

The little group were met at the station by Sister Sibyl who had been with Dolly when her mother died. Nonetheless, the sister did not acknowledge Dolly. The girls walked on up the road from the station each carrying her own bag and on arrival at the Eden Sanitorium were soon ushered to their room. Seeing them settled Miss Arbuthnot made her way to the nearby Alice Villa Hotel, where she would rest for a few days in the invigorating high mountain air, before returning to the heat of Calcutta.

Maggie and Dolly thrived in the fresh mountain air, gazing in wonder on clear mornings at the wonderful views glimpsed at sunrise, each peak lighting up in turn, bathing Kanchenjunga, the world's third highest peak, in pale pastel hues. The noise, heat and dust of Calcutta seemed far away in this land above the clouds. With each day Dolly's strength grew, as her sadness lessened, though at bedtime she still held her silver rattle close, praying and wishing that her father would come for her, soon, and hoping they could be together again. Tears stained her now rose-coloured cheeks as she drifted off into a dream-filled sleep.

CHAPTER 15
Calcutta
1889 - 1900

Alice Comely wrote regularly to Sister Sibyl in Darjeeling, enquiring after her two little charges. The replies from Darjeeling though few, were encouraging, so Alice decided to go ahead with her plans for Dolly and Maggie, to continue their education at the Mission in Kalimpong.

Back in 1889, Dr Graham from Edinburgh, had arrived in India with his new bride Katherine, via Switzerland, Austria and Italy. They sailed from Venice, changing ships at Suez and arriving in Calcutta on 21st March. The next day, he preached his first sermon in India, in the Scots Kirk in Dalhousie Square. The Grahams were guests of a Mr and Mrs Smith, missionaries working in Calcutta, and friends of Dr and Mrs Comley. Suddenly and unexpectedly Mrs Smith died within a fortnight of the Grahams arrival. Undaunted however, Mr Smith decided to accompany the Grahams on their journey to Darjeeling.

First by train to Siliguri, then with all their provisions on pack ponies, they continued on horseback through the forest tracks and tea gardens until they reached Darjeeling. They fell in love with this same view of Kanchenjunga which some eight years later young Dolly would first see. Neither would tire of its beauty, its majesty at dawn and sunset, the snow-capped peaks reaching up to heaven. Overnighting in Darjeeling, they set off the next morning on the last stage of the Grahams' seven-week journey from Edinburgh.

Cautiously the horses and pack ponies descended to the valley floor and along the bank of the Teesta River. A fast-flowing river even before the onset of the monsoon, becoming then a raging torrent. Eventually passing through rain forest and paddy fields on the other side of the valley they climbed higher finding the air thinner but hazy with charcoal smoke from a straggling collection of little huts huddled below the higher-level ridge of Kalimpong. Cloud shrouded this remote village high above the world. The shrill sound of cicadas and howling jackals filled the air, a far cry from the familiar sounds of 'Auld Reekie', their home town of Edinburgh. It was here, wedged between Bhutan and Sikkim, among exotically beautiful countryside and friendly Mongolian looking people, though with kukris in their belts, that Dr Graham's dream of a school was born.

From early days the area's tea plantations had been managed by young men recruited in Britain by the East India Company, who then found themselves isolated, living in poor quarters and with no near neighbours, seemingly 'prisoners' on the estates. Hence, many developed relationships with their women workers - a servant by day and a bed companion by night. When the tea planters moved district, the women were left behind along with the results of these relationships, mixed race children. Dr Graham became aware of these children during his travels around the plantations. The women and children were often kept out of sight of visitors, the planters not wishing to display their indiscretions. In spite of this, many felt obliged to have the children educated, rather than leaving them to run wild. Although some of the men were in mixed race marriages, acceptable in these regions, it would not have been acceptable at home in Britain or in other parts of India. The suffering and neglect of the illegitimate children was a delicate problem to Victorians. However monetary help from Britain was needed to allow Graham's plans to found a school, to educate and train these Eurasian children, and ease consciences.

Eventually in 1900 St Andrew's Colonial and Industrial Settlement was conceived.

Naming it St Andrew acknowledged the Scottish connection, and Colonial – to prepare the children for emigration to the Colonies.

CHAPTER 16
Kalimpong, India
1900

Since their meeting in 1889 Alice Comley and Dr Graham had corresponded regularly. Eventually in August 1900, with his school founded, she asked Dr Graham if he would take two of her little girls, Maggie Leslie and Dolly Higgins to complete their education at Kalimpong. She could pay Rs 10 monthly for Maggie but could only clothe Dolly, there not being sufficient money left for her continuing care. The Rs 150 gifted by William Higgins from his brother Frederick's estate had gone towards her care in St Mary's. Further strain had been put on the Home's finances due to the repair work following the earthquake. Hoping he would take Dolly without payment, in the hope she would eventually be sponsored, both girls could then continue with their education. Considering herself their guardian, Alice hoped that someday they would return to visit her, should she still be alive, and that throughout their time in the Homes she wished to be kept informed of their progress. Advising Dr Graham that both children were at the Eden Sanatorium in Darjeeling recuperating, Alice wondered if he could arrange for them to continue on to Kalimpong, saying that she would settle any expense with Sister Sibyl.

In September 1900 she once again thanked Dr Graham for writing and told him that she had asked Sister Sybil to keep the girls until October, the time he had said he would be able to have them brought over from Darjeeling. The Sister would then hand over their few belongings and a lump sum of Rs 1500 to cover all expenses. Unfortunately, with much sickness about and no-one able to collect the children, Dolly and Maggie stayed on in Darjeeling over the winter, eventually travelling back by train to Calcutta, along with an English lady, a Mrs McBride, who was returning home to England.

It was not till the beginning of May the following year and the start of the 1901 monsoon season that Dolly now nearly ten and Maggie a year younger, said a tearful goodbye to Alice Comley and St Mary's Homes, setting off at last on their journey to the trading town of Kalimpong, nestling high in the foothills of the Himalayas, on the Silk Road from the East. One of the ladies from St Mary's acted as chaperone escorting them on the train to Ghoom Junction where Dolly and Maggie were then taken in Dandy chairs on the backs of Coolies, with an attendant ayah for the last part of their dramatic journey. The little group descended to the Teesta Valley floor to ascend once more through rain forest, tea gardens and paddy fields to reach the awe-inspiring views from the east Indian hill town of Kalimpong, perched at over 4,000ft on a curving ridge high above the Teesta River. The town was home to many colonial buildings, including the 1891 MacFarlane Memorial Church, built with the help of local labour and dedicated to the first missionary.to visit Kalimpong, a William McFarlane of the Church of Scotland. He was later knighted, being the first missionary to set up a school in the area, for the benefit of the poor local Tibetan community.

The church sitting high in the cool air and with lovely gardens, had breath-taking views of mount Kanchenjunga. South of the town, was the hilltop Durpin Monastery, or Zang Dhok Palri Phodang, containing sacred Buddist scriptures. Deola Park also had lovely gardens with views of the town and surrounding hills. At the other end of the market town and on up the Deolo Hill lay the St Andrew's Colonial Mission, initiated by Dr Graham on his return to India in 1898 as St Andrew's Colonial and Industrial Settlement, providing the illegitimate and abandoned children of the tea planters, with a Christian home.

In 1900 Dr Graham founded St Andrew's Colonial Home, later renamed as Dr Graham Homes, which would become Dolly's home for the next eleven years.

CHAPTER 17
Children in Need
Kalimpong, India 1901

A remote Himalayan outpost of the British Empire bordering Bhutan and Sikkim, a life far away from a colonial centre, and thirty-one miles from Darjeeling, a place where you had to be self-sufficient. A modest, rented cottage on the bare hillside was the first home for six children from the Assam tea gardens. Dolly and Maggie were early admissions, and soon there were thirty-five children. Eventually the little cottage was bursting at the seams. Dr Graham's vision of a hillside dotted with cottages, a school, a farm and eventually a church, would form a little model village. This was to be no austere, loveless Victorian orphanage, but a home full of light and love. However, Victorian attitudes to the problems of poor Eurasian and Anglo-Indian children prevailed, and followed many of the Kalimpong students throughout their lives.

Children had been taken from, and denied both a father's and mother's love and concern. There was to be no identification with India, the country of their birth and those who benefited from the education and further training at the Home, would eventually be sent on to the colonies. Their parents and Indian heritage, long forgotten, a thing of the past. Dr Graham felt strongly that the plight of the children was indeed a British responsibility, and especially for many of the tea garden children, a Scottish responsibility. This white Christian environment the children found themselves in, led many to believe they had been born in Edinburgh, Scotland, and Dolly throughout her adult life always put her place of birth as Edinburgh.

Dr Graham travelled around India, begging bowl in hand, calling on the many rich British business men who were making fortunes from tea, jute and engineering. Such was his success that only six months after Dolly's arrival a second cottage was opened, and the foundation stone for another laid. A school, a nursery, a hospital, workshops and a farm slowly developed and still the children came, from Chittagong, Calcutta, Bombay, Bangalore, Assam, Darjeeling, Cawnpore and Allahabad, with more and more cottages needed. Each cottage had two British born house parents, non-smokers and abstainers, and with up to thirty children in their charge, the work was daunting.

Life for Dolly had changed beyond all recognition. Although she lived a somewhat carefree, barefoot existence in the open spaces of the barren hillside with an abundance of clean fresh air, the strict Victorian discipline meted out by staff and older children in the cottages, kept the young ones such as Dolly, at the bottom of the social hierarchy, a far cry from her early years in Calcutta. Her life became a series of duties; water-carrying, sweeping, cleaning, washing, cooking and wood-gathering, along with normal school lessons, and so at the end of the day there was little time to relax and play.

Life in the cottages was hard, both physically and mentally, but this would hopefully equip the children to survive later in a changing world, far from the isolated, sheltered existence in the Himalayas.

CHAPTER 18

Coal Creek,
West Coast,
New Zealand
1926 - 1928

Life in Kalimpong had been hard, equipping Dolly well for life at Coal Creek. In 1926 she moved from Christchurch to Coal Creek in response to an advert for a housekeeper to a Sydney Stewart a widower, a dairy farmer of Scottish decent, whose grandfather was from Kirriemuir, Angus in Scotland, and his own father from Sydney, New South Wales. Life for Dolly once again was a treadmill of sweeping, cleaning, water carrying, washing and cooking. Dolly and Sydney Stewart, scraped a meagre living off the land. The fire on Saturday 18th June 1927 gutted their farm steading and for a few months they had lived in the stable whilst Sydney rebuilt the wooden steading, replacing the corrugated iron roof.

During this time Dolly and six-year-old son Doug trudged into Greymouth to the hospital to visit baby Nancy as her condition worsened. Sadly, she died of pneumonia, a result of the burns. Her father took his grief and anger out on Doug, blaming him for the fire, which he couldn't understand as he felt it had nothing to do with him. Doug had been playing outside in the last of the daylight, before coming in, his father had been bedding the cows down after milking, while his mother had been preparing the evening meal. Lying in a Plunket cot in the small living room baby Nancy was asleep in front of the open coal fire.

Doug had come inside and was running about playing between the kitchen and the living room. Dolly asked him not to be noisy as he would waken Nancy, before it was time for her feed. Instead, asking him to go and sit quietly with his baby sister till his dinner was ready. Doug normally happy and content to play away by himself, scowled and muttered, as he ran through into the living room out of his mother's sight. Dolly aware that all had become quiet, with no chattering to baby Nancy, she continued preparing the vegetables. Suddenly, looking round, seeing Doug, his face ashen, standing, staring wide eyed up at her, saying nothing. The baby's screams broke the silence, and flickering light from the now visible flames lit the winter darkened passageway between the kitchen and baby Nancy. Realisation struck Dolly, dropping her knife she ran towards the flames, adrenalin propelling her, fear and panic overwhelming her.

It took some effort to smother Nancy's flanlette gown and lift her out of the cot, but Dolly was unable to stop the fire spreading, Nancy was foremost in her mind. White with fright, and with Doug crying at her heels and mumbling sorry, sorry, she quickly handed the baby to Doug saying she wouldn't be a minute, she ran back into the kitchen soon reappearing, and taking Nancy from Doug she ran as fast as she could across the paddock clutching the screaming baby to her bosom. Dolly reached the Williams' farmstead; her cries having warned them of her panicking approach with Mrs Williams already phoning the fire brigade and doctor. Hearing the screams Sydney ran from the byre, but parts of the steading were already lost to the fire.

Dr McKay arrived, but did not think the injuries to Nancy's face and hands were serious enough to take her to Greymouth hospital. He made two more visits to the farm on Monday 20th and Thursday 23rd following, and considered Nancy's condition satisfactory. On the Friday, a week after the accident, Nancy stopped feeding and was breathing with difficulty. Realising their daughter needed immediate medical help, Dolly and Sydney took her to the Grey Hospital, where she was admitted. Her condition deteriorated as she developed sceptic pneumonia, a complication

of the burns, and she died on Thursday 7th July. She was 5 months old. Sydney had now lost two baby daughters.

An inquest was held at Greymouth on Friday 8th July 1927 before Acting Coroner, Mr F. H. Kilgour, concerning the death of Nancy Elizabeth Mary Stewart, the five months old daughter of Mr and Mrs S. Stewart, of Coal Creek, who died at the Grey Hospital on

the 7th July as the result of burns. Having heard the witness Mrs S Stewart say, that she did not think that the boy had been interfering with the baby or the fire, a verdict was returned in accordance with the medical evidence, that death was due to burns received by accident. The jury members expressed their sympathy with the bereaved parents. A dark cloud hung over the

little family. However, on Monday 29th October 1928 young Sid was born. Doug loved his little half-brother watching over him, and playing with him when he came home from school. He also helped his mother around the house and garden, mostly keeping out of the way of his step-father.

Sid was eight months old when the Buller Earthquake struck.

CHAPTER 19

The Murchison/Buller Earthquake, New Zealand
17th June 1929

The earthquake on Monday 17th June 1929 was felt the length of New Zealand's South Island, devastating the Murchison area and causing widespread damage throughout the Buller District. For days before, booming noises were heard in the hills around, with slight tremors being felt in the early hours of the morning though creating no great alarm,
New Zealand hadn't earned the name 'The Shaky Isles' for nothing, so young Doug had gone off to school as usual. At 10.17am the intense shaking started, centred in the sparsely populated, mountainous, densely wooded area, north of Coal Creek. Extensive landslides were triggered over an area extending thousands of square miles, from Greymouth, north to Cape Farewell and east to Nelson. Roads, bridges, and buildings were severely damaged, fifteen people were killed, overwhelmed by the numerous slips sweeping away the steep slopes. As a result of blocked rivers and waterways 38 new lakes were formed, of which Lake Stanley survives. Thunderous reverberations from the rocking, heaving earth, drowned out the sound of the creaking and groaning of houses, the clattering of falling movables and the crashing of chimneys onto and through rooftops.

Dolly had difficulty keeping her feet as she picked up baby Sid from the new wood and canvas cot Sidney had made. She ran outside, stumbling. She felt queasy and shocked. Crouching beside the cowshed, she cradled Sid close to her, trying to comfort him – and herself. Strong shakes were succeeded by loud detonations which continued throughout the day and well into the night. Fearful and cautious, people did not go back into their homes, sheltering instead in sheds and tents.

Sydney and Dolly eventually made their way to the school playground where they found Doug and the reassuring comfort of the many others who had gathered there. Eventually they were given something to eat and drink at the hastily assembled open-air kitchen. From the playground they saw that the hills around their fertile flats, were stripped to bare rock, and great fissures appeared along the river bank. The Gray River bridge was impassable, due to the build-up of debris which had been carried down from higher ground. Power lines and telegraph poles were down, hence there was no communication, except for a few wireless receiving sets; no lights, the local main generator in the nearby power house having been wrenched from its bearings. People from neighbouring valleys having struggled into Greymouth, told of relatives and friends buried in their homes engulfed by the landslides. Miles of roads had vanished; lakes had risen behind dams of debris across rivers, and people were terrified of further disaster.

Rock choked rivers burst their banks resulting in flooding, in many cases worse than the earthquake damage. The results of ongoing slips were non-stop over the coming week, leaving Westport in isolation. News was sent by wireless from a ship in Greymouth harbour and by the next day Tiger Moth aeroplanes with wireless operators from Christchurch, landed on the beach at Westport, soon re-establishing communications between Westport to the north, Reefton to the east and Greymouth to the west. Weeks and months passed and repair work continued throughout the Murchison area, on roads, railway lines, bridges, tunnels, water supplies and sewage pipes, and with the winter rain continuing, there were many more landslides along the west coast.

Returning home later that first day, Sydney and Dolly were thankful to find little damage to their property. After settling the boys, Dolly checked for the white cotton drawstring bag with the little silver rattle, and relieved, found it still safely in the drawer. Patting it softly, she wondered why she had kept it, as there had been many times she could have sold it for much needed money. So many years had passed since those days in Calcutta, how her life and her name had changed. She often wondered if it had all really happened. Today had brought back memories of another earthquake, and how it had changed her life. She had never seen her father again, didn't even know if he had survived the quake, but surely, he would have come for her if he had, she often wondered. Maybe that was why she kept the little rattle just to let herself know that once she really had been loved and cared for, but how it had all changed.

Having just recovered from the fire, Sydney and Dolly were grateful that there had been little damage to the house this time, though for some time aftershocks would still be felt. Douglas continued at school and young Sid grew and thrived. Dolly worked the fields close to the homestead, creating reminders of a life long ago in Kalimpong. She baked and shopped for provisions, while Sydney chopped trees for fuel, tended the cows, and horses, also keeping the house, stable and cowshed watertight, the West Coast being subject to a high rainfall.

So, life continued in Coal Creek Flat and then on Monday 17th April 1933 Dolly at the age of 42 years gave birth to her last child, another girl, Virginia.

CHAPTER 20
Douglas James Higgins
Coal Creek Flat
1935

The sound of a green plumaged bell bird on the tree outside the little attic window wakened Douglas early. Taking a few minutes to come to, he remembered it was his birthday. The 21st May and early winter. Doug felt that it would not be a very special day, he was now 14 and growing fast, and soon he would be leaving school and looking for work. Dolly he hoped would be baking him a sponge cake for his birthday tea as usual, and giving him a kiss and a hug and ruffling his thick, wavy, auburn hair. Perhaps just a hug this year now he was growing up. Doug had been two years and nine months in February 1924 when they had moved from Nelson, leaving the new baby behind with a kind, older lady. Dolly had taken the train from Nelson to Still-Water Junction with their few belongings, in response to the advert for a housekeeper on a farm in Coal Creek Flat. A Sydney Stewart had advertised for a housekeeper, deciding to take Dolly on not only to work in the house but also to help on the farm. On arrival and in the following days, Dolly kept Doug close to her trying to keep him out of Sydney's way as best she could. Sydney was a hardworking man of few words, having been on his own since his wife Catherine Rose, and baby daughter Virginia Rose had died, many years before. Grateful that he had given them a roof over their head and asked few questions, Dolly worked hard. Their relationship developed, and Dolly found herself pregnant. Syd and she married in Greymouth on the 9th September 1926.

Not long after the wedding, Sydney headed off down the coast to his batch, which he did every year for the whitebait season. Taking his horse and cart down the coast to fill up with whitebait, selling the fish locally, later taking whitebait back for spreading on the fields, and also with enough left for a tasty meal. Dolly being left on her own, fended as best she could on the farm with spring fast approaching. November saw the end of white baiting, in time for summer. Doug was growing up fast, enjoying the freedom of running about in the fields and helping his stepfather at milking time. Dolly's pregnancy moved along and soon it was June, time for the baby to be born. Their neighbour, the kindly Mrs Williams and local midwife, helped with the birth of baby Nancy, everything going smoothly. Sydney returned home to find his baby daughter lying peacefully in the Plunket cot he had made, with young Doug sitting cross-legged close by watching his new little sister, and Dolly preparing the evening meal. With the arrival of the new baby Sydney planned improvements to the farmstead to make life a little easier. Updating the water supply and installing a generator, would certainly improve their life. Most of the work was complete when their home was almost burnt to the ground. Not only did they lose their shelter, but tragically baby Nancy.

Dolly became withdrawn, rarely speaking, it was as if she saw or heard no-one. Young Doug was terribly upset and cried a lot making Sydney very angry. So much so that he shouted at him, sending him out of the way to the stable. Later his stepfather dragged him from the stable, thrashing him many times, oblivious to the young boy's screaming, still blaming him for baby Nancy's death. His mother lived on in her own silent world, Doug creeping about quietly keeping out of his step father's way. Walking to school and back on his own, playing around the stable or in the paddock. At mealtimes no one spoke, never asking him how he had got on at school. He was very much alone.

They had lived as best they could in the newly built hut beside the stable, however, Syd eventually with the help of a few neighbours rebuilt the little farm steading and soon they moved back in. Life was never the same again for young Doug, feeling a great sadness that his mother had not protected him against Syd's wrath, especially as Doug felt he had not caused the fire or baby Nancy's death. He had always wondered why his mother had screamed at him to take the baby outside while she herself ran back into the house, seemingly oblivious to the flames, shouting that she had to save the rattle. Why save a rattle when they themselves, their home and new baby were in such danger, he never understood.
When Dolly came out, taking Nancy from Doug she ran to the neighbours to telephone for the Doctor and the fire brigade. Sydney always blamed Doug for the fire, through his carelessness.

Once again, by 1928 they had a roof over their head, and in June, Doug had a new baby brother, Sidney.

CHAPTER 21

Coal Creek, New Zealand
21st May 1935

Doug whistled as he made his way home from school that Tuesday afternoon, he had had a good day, playing football with some of the boys from his class at lunchtime in the nearby paddock. Soon his school days would be over, he felt good. It was his birthday, and his mother would have baked him a birthday sponge. He and young Sid would enjoy sharing it, maybe Virginia too.

With one hand on the post, he leaped the fence at their road end and ran along the rough path skipping and scuffing stones till he reached the farm house. He pushed open the door calling out for his mother, but there was no reply. There was no kitchen light on and no smell of fresh baking. Realising that the house was empty, fear gripped him. No mother, no Sid, no young Virginia, and where was his step-father? Doug was alone and scared. He ran outside, to the hut, the stable, to the cowshed, no sign of anyone there either. Where was his mother? He called out for her. 'She's gone', came the gruff reply from behind him. Knowing the voice, Doug swung round ready to protect himself. 'Took the children a while ago and off she went, not a word, who the hell does she think she is? There's work to be done, she's caused me too much bother already, so I don't really care where she's gone. Go and pack your things, you're not even mine, birthday or no birthday, away with you, get out of my sight, it's time you earned your own living. Maybe she left to catch the train from Greymouth, I don't know, that's about a couple of hours ago now. If she didn't come for you, well, guess she didn't want you either. Best head off on your own to wherever you came from, bugger-off and get out of my sight, you're trouble like your mother."

Doug ran into the house stumbling passed the wooden table and chairs and on up to his attic room, packed a few clothes in an old rucksack and headed off, running back up the rough path to the main road, never looking back. His head throbbing, his heart beating wildly and tears filling his eyes, where would he go, what would he do, with only a shilling in his pocket? Doug didn't know where he came from; his mother had never told him. How could she leave him, only taking young Sid and the baby? Then he remembered that she had done this before, many years ago, taken him, but leaving the baby Hector with a much older woman, who had come to the door answering the advert in the *Nelson Evening Mail; WANTED – kind lady to adopt healthy baby boy, 2 weeks old, Apply 5 Washington Road.* As Doug had watched, clinging on to his mother's skirt, Dolly handed baby Hector over to the grey-haired lady. Ethel Crichton had a kind face and smiled down at Douglas who edged away behind his mother, frightened she would take him away too. Doug quietly sobbed, confused by all that was going on, not understanding. Not long after giving the baby away, Dolly and Doug had left the white, wooden, house where she had cleaned and cooked for the elderly man who was fond of Doug, having watched him grow from a small baby. He had also encouraged Dolly to enjoy gardening. With what little money she had saved Dolly headed south west from Nelson by train to Still-Water Junction to be met by her new employer, in answer to the advert in the Grey River Argos, *WANTED Housekeeper, Coal Creek Flat. S. Stewart.* So, with these thoughts in his mind Doug ran along the rough verge of the main road before cutting across the paddock behind the school, where earlier he had enjoyed playing football and on towards the river.

Dolly arrived home later that afternoon with young Sid carrying a parcel and Dolly carrying young Virginia. Doug was nowhere to be seen; she had been hoping to surprise him with the new pair of boots she had bought from the store in Greymouth. Glancing up from his paper Syd paused, then said that Doug had been in earlier but had run off saying he had somewhere to go and he hadn't seen him since, 'must be an hour or so ago now'. Dolly went up to the boys' room and found the rucksack from the hook behind the door gone, along with some of Douglas's clothes, her heart sinking and her stomach heaving. She sat on the bed gathering herself together, before going back down the wooden stair and into the kitchen. She never spoke, but began to fill the kettle for Virginia's tea-time feed then, searching out potatoes, a few vegetables and some cold chicken for their meal, before sitting in the chair next to the fire to feed a hungry Virginia. No one spoke. Young Sid sat at his mother's feet, drawing a little card for Doug.

Finding it later, his father tore it up and flung it in the fire.

CHAPTER 22
Coal Creek to Westport, New Zealand
1935

The way to Nelson, Doug's first idea, was long, far longer than the coastal route to Westport on Buller Bay, at the mouth of the Buller River, after it flows through the Lower Buller Gorge. The only other place with a working harbour Doug knew about was Greymouth, not far from Coal Creek at the mouth of the Grey River, but that was too near to home, and someone might recognise him. Especially as recently he had been involved in a cycling accident on the main highway at Coal Creek, the other casualty a forty-year-old man was admitted, unconscious, to Gray Hospital having sustained head injuries and concussion. Doug had escaped with minor abrasions, along with a sharp warning from the police, followed by a crack across the head by Syd, when he returned home. Dolly was stunned by Sid's reaction but said nothing. This was the second accident Doug had been involved in, the first a few years ago when he was much younger, and now she was beginning wonder if Syd's thoughts about Doug were right.

There was always work at a wharf and Doug was tall and well-built for his age, so Westport it would be. Following the road along part of the Grey River, then skirting the tail end of the Rapahoe Range, along the edge of Cobden and the Lagoon, and on to the coastal path heading north to Point Elizabeth Lookout. Somewhere around Rapahoe he planned to spend the night. Someone would give a boy a bite to eat he was sure, along with a corner of their barn to bed down. He would set off at first light. He wondered, this being his birthday, if his mother would miss him - maybe not, she had let him down before. Seldom sticking up for him against Syd Stewart, that hurt. He would miss young Sid though, who would be wondering where his big brother was, and even Virginia, his two-year-old sister might miss him.

The winding coastal path along the foot of the hills was steep in parts, with bare rock from the '29 earthquake still exposed. New young tree ferns were clinging to parts of the hillside again and four years of fresh undergrowth made the walking difficult. Little bellbirds flitted around Doug's knees, catching the insects disturbed as he trudged along. Tuis called from high branches, raindrops splashed off the tree ferns, Doug realised he would need to find shelter soon. It seemed a long way to Westport especially on your own, but that was where he was going. It looked as if he had little choice, he would run away to sea and be a fisherman or a boy sailor.

Good-bye Mother said a tiny lad,
I'm going now to join my dad'
He wouldn't take me, a sailor to make me
So, I'll run away.
Stow away, stow away,
My heart keeps saying to me
Go away, go away,
And be a sailor.

Anon

CHAPTER 23

Daily Life
Kalimpong, India
1906

*"Let us with a gladsome mind
Praise the Lord for he is kind,"*

Set in one of the most charming valleys of the Himalayas, with gentle cultivated slopes, rich gold in autumn and varying shades of green in early spring, and edged with long sweeping circles of snowy peaks, separating Kalimpong from Tibet. The trade route was busy with wool-laden mules, their decorative bells tinkling, and attended by exotic looking herdsmen, from lands beyond the mighty barrier. At a height of over 4,000ft the region is beyond the reach of malaria, the high ridge of Kalimpong sheltering the area from the northbound monsoon current and unlike other mountain sides, mist free.

Already parts of the hillside were dotted with eight cottages, a farm steading, workshops, a central school, play sheds, and soon a hospital and sanatorium would be added to complete the village. A clock tower was also being erected as the central focus for the Homes. Although the children lived in cottages. the buildings were actually double storied villas accommodating up to 30 children. There was a kitchen range, with a scullery off the dining room, which was large enough to sit all the children and the two house parents. The upper floor was taken up by roomy dormitories.

The children's day began at 6.00am with breakfast followed by house duties till 9.00am. They then went to school, to the workshops or the farm. Each child had their appointed task in the mornings before Central School, and duties too at lunch time. They stayed at school till 4.00pm in the afternoon followed by an hour of play, then tea and bed. Every day there was a kitchen boy and girl who stayed on in the cottage, working and cleaning up, and on Saturday mornings, washing day, boys as well as girls learnt the 'art' of laundry. On weekend afternoons the children went for rambles, played games, or carried out voluntary work in the township of Kalimpong. On Sundays mornings after finishing house duties, the children went to Sunday school, then in the afternoon they walked to Kalimpong to attend the church service there and finishing with an evening Christian Endeavour meeting. Under strict Presbyterian discipline, Dolly's barefoot life continued at Woodburn Cottage, with work and schooling, and although love was preached it wasn't always practiced.

The first building in the compound was Woodburn Cottage opened in 1901 by the Lt. Governor of Bengal, Sir John Woodburn. Work continued with a new cottage each year; Elliot 1902, Calcutta 1903, Strachan 1904, Thorburn 1905, Bene 1906, Lucia King 1910, Macgregor 1912, Scottish Canadian 1912 and then the Edinburgh cottage in 1915.

In the first eight years the numbers of children grew from 72 in 1902 to 305 in 1910. The barren hillside becoming a children's village, a working settlement. Anniversaries, Holiday Days and also Fun Picnics in May brightened up the usual routine when the school broke up for its two-week holiday. Dolly, along with the rest of the children, looked forward to this time. Enjoying rambling over the hillsides along with the other girls from Woodburn cottage, gathering ferns, orchids or trying to catch butterflies. On May afternoons each cottage would hold a picnic. It was a steep climb to the top of the hill behind Woodburn cottage for their picnic, the other cottages held their picnics on the lower grounds around the village.

A happy time was had by all, with singing and dancing, playing tennis and badminton. The House Parents happily joined in too, it was a change from their usual rigid routine. Preparations for the picnics started early the previous day, with the housemothers and children cooking and baking. Cooked meat was made into a great pie, the batter pudding was baked in large tins for easy carrying, then cut into slices for serving the next day. Milk from their own cows, providing a refreshing drink. There were cakes and biscuits, bread and butter, all packed and ready to go the next day after breakfast and prayers.

A fire was lit at the picnic spot and kerosene tins full of water were set on the fire to boil for tea for the grown-ups. Meanwhile the boys played at rounders, the girls enjoyed skipping and singing, the time passing quickly till at three o'clock when everything was finished and tidied up, they set off back to their cottage. Tired but very happy.

The second week held the greatest excitement, a trip to the Haat Bazaar in Kalimpong, usually forbidden ground. The bustling village market was held every Wednesday and Saturday between 7.00am and 6.00pm. Traders from the surrounding area came and set up stalls to sell their goods. The market was popular and a true experience of local flavours and colours. The stall holders sold clothes, umbrellas, bags and sandals on one side of the street and fruits, vegetables, local and agricultural produce and colourful spices on the other. The children always wanted to get there early to try out the tasty local delicacies, before the favourite things were sold out. It was a local tradition where people came together and Kalimpong came alive.

As Dolly settled into this way of life the world outside seemed more and more distant. Teachers came and went, as did House Parents, some so strict in their own upbringing and manner, that beatings were not unknown. However, despite the harshness of the regime, the system was respected far beyond the boundaries of Kalimpong, and this became the only life Dolly really knew, following her eventually into the outside world far beyond the Himalayas and the Indian continent..

She was provided for by faceless people who prided themselves in their Christian giving.

CHAPTER 24
Coal Creek Flat to Christchurch
1938

*"There had come back from Germany to
Downing Street peace with honour.
I believe it is peace in our time."* Neville Chamberlain

As the German Army marched into Austria in March 1938 and seven months later crossed the border into Czechoslovakia, King George V1 and his Consort, Queen Elizabeth opened the Empire Exhibition in Bellahouston Park, Glasgow, Dolly was given her marching orders from Coal Creek Flat. Virginia was five years old and Sidney ten years old when they left the farm to travel from Still Water to Christchurch by train, Dolly had 10/- in her pocket.

*And THIS after years of devotion,
After countless sleepless nights,
After heartaches innumerable,
After spending every halfpenny, I ever had on her
This is my reward.
Oh woman…Fickle woman!*

Anon

The second fire started again in the living room but this time in the chimney, filling the room with smoke and soon spread through the house. Rushing from the garden towards the front steps onto the narrow wooden veranda, Dolly shouted on Sydney to come quickly. Swearing at the top of his voice, he pushed passed Dolly knocking her to the veranda floor.

'Go and get Mrs Williams to phone for the fire brigade, or all will

be lost this time, you fool', he shouted, 'I gave you and your bastard a home, look how you've treated it, - all your life others have provided for you, looked after you, what do you care, – just get out!'
Struggling to her feet Dolly tried to steady herself, but the next blow from Sydney's fist struck her on the side of the head, sending her scrambling against the wooden railing. Grabbing on to the rail, she managed to keep her balance, and entering the smoke-filled kitchen, stumbled to the dresser recovering the little lace edged dolly-bag, quickly putting it in her pocket, then gasping she ran from the burning house heading for their neighbour. By the time she reached the Williams's house she was out of breath and could hardly speak, her whole body shaking, her face bruised. The neighbours having seen the pall of smoke had already called the fire brigade, but it was too far and too late by the time they arrived.

Dolly gratefully accepted the hot sweet tea, and sitting with the mug in her trembling hands, she was comforted by Mrs Williams's quiet words of wisdom. Dolly knew she could not go back. She was relieved Sid and Virginia were at school, but what would they do now, where could she go? Putting down the mug she felt in her apron pocket, for the little rattle, it was still there with the 10/- note. With all she stood up in, it was all she had in the world. She buried her face in her hands and wept.

After the fire engine had left, Sydney Stewart stood staring at the smoking remains of his home. Where would he find the energy, the money, to start over again? All he had too, was what he stood up in. He cursed the day he had let Dolly Higgins or Doreen as he knew her, into his life.

Laughing and shouting Sid and Virginia ran out of school, happy to be making their way home. In the distance they saw the billowing smoke.
'Wow Mum has a big fire on today!' they both said together.
Mrs Williams ran out of the front door and on up to the road

calling on the children to come with her as Mum was in her house waiting for them. The expectation of a slice of homemade chocolate cake and a glass of milk hurried the two children on their way. Coming in to Mrs William's house, both a bit out of breath with all their running, Dolly hugged them. Sitting them down beside her, then as best she could, told the now alarmed children what had happened, adding that Mrs Williams had offered them a roof and a bed for the night. The following morning, Dolly would decide what was to be done. After a meal of lamb stew and warm homemade bread and butter washed down by fresh milk, the little family settled down for the night in Mrs Williams's attic room. Dolly lay on the old sofa with a rug over her, trying to sort out some sort of plans for herself and the children, exhausted she eventually fell asleep.

Having finally decided they would take the early afternoon train from Greymouth to Christchurch the following day, boarding at Still-Water Junction. The five-hour journey would take them over the mountainous spine of South Island with the backdrop of the Southern Alps, rather than the Himalayas, crossing the aqua blue Waimakariri River, through Arthur's Pass before traversing the majestic Canterbury Plain, with its tussock fields and viaducts before arriving in Christchurch - which Dolly remembered from years before when she was in service there. The 10/- note in her pocket would go only a little way to help.

Later the next morning, filled with toast, jam and steaming mugs of hot tea and with a few belongings in a bag which Mrs Williams had looked out for them, along with sandwiches and apples for the long journey, they set out for the station. Thanking Mrs Williams many times for all her help and support over the years, Dolly and the children clambered into the back of Mr Williams's farm wagon, and waved goodbye. Mr Williams slipped Dolly enough money for her ticket and some extras when he dropped them at the station, suggesting the children could hide in the toilet whilst the guard checked the tickets. In years to come their fears on the day would be a source of fun.

Dolly had lived in Coal Creek Flat for twelve years, a year longer than in Kalimpong, with about as much love. She had felt then that she belonged nowhere and now the same feelings overwhelmed her again.

CHAPTER 25

Christchurch - Revisited
1938

The little family reached the platform as train was about to pull out of Still-Water, the guard shouting for them to hurry. Sid helped his mother up with her bag after having helped Virginia up into the train before jumping up himself, just as the train lurched forward. They found seats in the nearest compartment as the train wasn't busy. Ignoring the quizzical looks from other passengers, Dolly settled herself, putting her arm around Virginia, with Sid sitting opposite looking out of the window, watching and wondering if he would ever see his father, or the farm again. The train soon gathered speed as it left the Junction, bound for Christchurch on the other side of South Island.

Half an hour into the journey Dolly became aware of the guard making his rounds. Quietly telling the children to follow her and without any fuss, managed to hide them in the toilet at the far end of the carriage, before returning to her seat. After paying the guard for her ticket Dolly fortunately had some change left, enough for an evening paper. A chance then to look for a job, and along with the extra money Mr Williams had given her there would be enough to see them through their first few days. After the guard passed on through the carriage Virginia went back for Sid and Virginia, who were fine, if a little giggly. Settling back again into their seats, Virginia and Sid looked excitedly out of the window pointing at the magnificent Southern Alps, seeing them for the first time.

After enjoying Mrs Williams' sandwiches, Virginia cuddled close to her mother, who kept an eye out for the guard. Fortunately, he never returned, and the rest of the long trip was trouble free. The children snuggled into their mother while Dolly gazed out of the window as they journeyed through Arthur's Pass and down onto the vast expanse of the Canterbury Plain. Reflecting that Virginia was now five, the age Dolly was when she travelled from Darjeeling to Calcutta with her father, after her mother had died. A lifetime away. Dolly closed her eyes, losing herself in her memories. Surely this time things would work out. Lulled by the sounds and rhythm of the train, Dolly slept. The next few hours passed peacefully.

Arriving at Addington Station, Christchurch, in the early evening, meant Dolly had little time to find somewhere to stay. Buying the evening paper, she quickly searched the jobs column for housekeeping posts. There were several vacancies, but few with accommodation suitable for herself and the children. The historic Carlton Hotel, on the corner of Papanui Road and Bealey Avenue seemed the most promising. The station at the southwestern edge of the city and Hagley Park, which Dolly remembered, meant quite a walk across the city with Sid and Virginia trotting behind. Their eyes wide as they took in their first sights of Christchurch in the dusk of evening. Built for the 1906 New Zealand International Exhibition the hotel had seen better days, but it looked clean, the curtains at the windows fresh, even in the evening light. Up the front step the little family went, through the revolving door into the dark wood panelled foyer. Two large potted ferns decorated the hallway, with two well-worn easy chairs and a small well-polished reception desk.

The receptionist in her early forties, whose smoothed bond hair was curled at the ends to frame her face, looked critically at Dolly over her glasses, though smiling at the two children. Dolly said she had come about the job advertised in the *Evening Chronicle*.

Asking Dolly to take a seat, she lifted the phone, spoke quietly for a few moments, and then looking over at Dolly saying that the Housekeeper, Mrs Hawkes, would see her shortly. Soon a stout woman in her early sixties, came through the door behind reception, and sat on the chair opposite Dolly. After introducing herself, and listening to Dolly's story. she offered to take her on a week's trial with accommodation but without the children. As Christchurch had several suitable children's homes, Mrs Hawkes suggested Dolly could contact them in the morning. Tonight, the three of them could share a room and she would see Dolly the following afternoon to start her shift.

After speaking to the housekeeper, the receptionist told Dolly there was a spare room on the top floor at the back of the building, it was small with a bed and a spare mattress which would do them for one night. Dolly could also have it for a few nights till she found her own accommodation. The Housekeeper then ushered the little family through to the kitchen where she made them hot milky drinks and put some biscuits on a plate. Eagerly Dolly, Sid and Virginia ate the sweet biscuits, and by the time they were finishing their cups of hot cocoa, their eyelids were drooping. After the long day travelling, Dolly and the children were indeed very tired but very grateful to have a bed for the night.

Tomorrow would look after itself.

CHAPTER 26

Christchurch, New Zealand
Nazareth House and St Joseph's Home for Boys
1938

Dolly woke early the next morning, washed herself and the children at the sink in the communal bathroom on the floor below. Feeling refreshed they went down to the kitchen to see if they could have something to eat. The breakfast cook, a middle-aged, grey-haired woman with smiling, dark brown eyes, made them toast and scrambled eggs along with mugs of hot sweet tea. Thanking the cook, Dolly and the children stood quietly over at the far end of the kitchen out of her way. A young waitress came through into the kitchen and taking the family into the dining room, showed them to a quiet corner table. She returned shortly with their breakfasts which they eagerly ate. After finishing, Dolly and the children went back upstairs to their room to gather their few belongings, then coming down to reception to ask the receptionist for directions to the homes. A few other guests had arrived down for breakfast by this time, and one or two were waiting in reception to pay their bill. The receptionist had kindly written out the addresses for Dolly on a piece of paper which she handed over. Thanking the receptionist for everything, and saying she would be back in the early afternoon, Dolly, Sid and Virginia said goodbye and set out for Nazareth House in Brougham Street, west of Sydenham Park. After hopefully getting Virginia settled, Dolly and Sid would then go on to St Joseph's Home for boys to see if there was a place there for him. Sad as it was to be separated after all they had gone through in the last few days, putting children in homes was something Dolly understood and although not ideal, she believed Virginia and Sid would be well looked after, well fed, and have a clean bed. Allowing her time to hopefully secure a job and find somewhere suitable to stay, before she went back for them.

Built thirty years earlier Nazareth House was used by the Sisters of Nazareth as an orphanage for unwanted, parentless babies and children. Its spartan interior was sunless belying the lively Gothic façade on Brougham Street. Behind the façade were impressive stairways, long corridors, classrooms and numerous dormitories. The dormitories on the second floor, were bare and airless, with narrow iron beds with thin mattresses and a single grey blanket. Virginia would however have a roof over her head, be fed and cared for, and would continue with her early school work. Dolly would keep in touch and then, and when she had found rooms, they would be together again. She could not have imagined that it would be spring before this would happen.

Dolly gave no thought to the fact that these Roman Catholic homes might not be sympathetic to Anglican children, but admitted them none the less.

CHAPTER 27

Nazareth House,
Brougham Street
Christchurch, New Zealand

Life was hard in Nazareth House. Rising herself at four thirty Sister Teresa prepared tea for the other sisters before rousing the community, and then the girls at five opening the dormitory door; and clapping her hands three times, signalling the start of a new day and loudly stating 'Christ is risen'! Time for the children to rise and dress, the younger ones like Virginia struggling; before walking, with their heads bowed, and palms pressed together in front of them, to the chapel for an hour before a breakfast of thick slices of bread, fruit and a glass of milk. They returned to the dormitories to make their beds, then marched to the washrooms before heading to the classrooms for the day's lessons.

Virginia, though not understanding the rituals, went to chapel taking communion along with the other girls, later being told that she should not have taken communion and was caned. Even walking in the grounds, most of the children knew to make the sign of the cross when passing statues of the Virgin Mary, also in the corridor alcoves. If you didn't, punishment was again with the cane. Virginia was frightened, upset and puzzled, not knowing what to do, never having experienced this before, so, damned if she did and damned if she didn't. Her chastisement most days was scrubbing the long stone corridors, and soon her knees and shins were red. raw and sore. She was not alone with this discipline; age making no difference. It seemed that every smile or word spoken out of turn, merited a reprimand. Virginia's greatest sins were her mother's sins, a single mother and Anglican.

Instead of protection, the girls were threatened with the fearful consequences which would befall them, if not now, then certainly in the hereafter. Screams were heard in the night, as doors opened and closed, followed with muffled weeping, as girls clung to their pillows for comfort. Virginia noticed, but could not understand, why some of the girls were sullen and withdrawn, holding back at playtime, not joining in skipping or playground games. Instead of gathering in little groups for girlish chatter, preferring to stand by themselves looking at the ground, or picking at their nails. There was a mystery surrounding these girls which Virginia did not understand. It aroused her curiosity.

Mary in the bed next to Virginia was one of these silent girls. Many times, her bed was empty when Virginia came back from the washroom in the evening. Yet, she was there in the morning, her eyes red, face puffed and pale. When Virginia asked her where she had been at bedtime, she stared vacantly. Noticing Mary always seemed to disappear after evening prayers, usually being held back by Sister Teresa, saying she needed further instruction. They would then disappear back along the corridor in the opposite direction from the dormitories. The other girls were marched smartly along, their hands clasped in front of them, heads bowed, never daring to look behind lest they felt the cane across their legs. What happened elsewhere was not their business. Virginia's curiosity got the better of her. One evening after supper when everyone went to chapel for the final blessing before the grand silence, as they left the chapel, un-noticed she slipped behind a statue and hid, until the crocodile of girls had passed along out of sight. She then slipped into the room where she knew Sister Theresa took Mary.

Virginia being small, managed to squeeze herself between the grandfather clock and an old armchair. She did not have long to wait till she heard the scuffling footsteps to stop outside. The room was in darkness. As the door opened, the light from the corridor illuminated the nun pushing the sobbing girl into the room. A lump formed in Virginia's throat, she held her chest with one hand and covered her mouth with the other. The fear was tangible. Pointing to the rug in front of the stone fireplace, the nun told Mary to lie down. Still sobbing the girl lay down and curled herself into a ball. Wide eyed Virginia watched horrified by the light of the fire as the nun peeled off her outer garment, then threw her pants onto the old arm chair. Sister Teresa then started fondling her own small breasts, moaning gently before moving over to where the frightened child lay. Nudging her over onto her back with her foot she then straddled her, sitting back on her heels, her body over the young girl's face, the nun rocking herself back and forth gasping loudly, before throwing her head back, eyes bulging, and staring blindly at the ceiling. She shouted, then sighing, collapsed to the floor. Struggling to get out from under her, and scrambling to her feet, Mary tried to escape. Sister Teresa was quick, grabbing her, she roughly pushed her over the desk. Ripping at Mary's clothes and picking up the cane she started whipping her, oblivious of her screams. Virginia's mind spinning as she eased herself out from behind the chair, stumbling and tripping before she reaching the door. Sister Theresa caught hold of Virginia and lashed out with the cane again in a frenzied manner, whipping her wildly, till exhausted the nun fell back onto the chair gasping.

Taking their chance to escape the girls ran to the door. In seconds they were in the empty corridor clinging to each other, before running as fast as they could to the washroom, Mary keeping hold of Virginia's hand. They managed to bathe the red weals and dabbed them dry with the rough towel that hung behind the washroom door. Creeping along the empty corridor to their dormitory, neither spoke a word. By the look in each other's eyes they knew they were bound together by a terrible secret. Both slept fitfully that night, rising at dawn with the same nun clapping her hands. Dressing, and following her to chapel, it started another day of praying for forgiveness, asking the Virgin Mary for guidance to give them peace in their hearts. Virginia prayed for her mother to come for her. There was so much she did not understand, she was too young, but she knew deep inside that what she had seen and heard was evil…suffer the little children… indeed many were suffering.

With only the occasional visit, it was six months before Dolly could come for Virginia to take her back to live with her again. She had now managed to rent a couple of rooms above a bakers shop in Durham Street.

It was here in early August 1941 when Virginia was eight, on coming home from school she found a young sailor sitting on the edge of her mother's bed. Dolly had been unwell and off work. On seeing the little girl, the sailor stood up, smiling, then said goodbye and left. Her mother told her that the sailor was her brother Hector, who was heading off to war. His adoptive mother Ethel Crichton, who had occasionally kept in touch with Dolly over the years, suggested that Hector go and see his mother before he went to war, not knowing when and if he would come back safely.

Dolly never met Hector again, and it was more than 50 years before Virginia was reunited with him.

CHAPTER 28

St Joseph's Home,
Middleton,
Riccarton,
Christchurch, New Zealand

St Joseph's Home for Boys was opened on Sunday the 17th April 1921 by his Lordship Bishop Brodie in the presence of a very large gathering. The Home was a two storied building, sitting in 80 acres with accommodation for 100 boys. The Catholic Church's aim was to plant religious education in the hearts of the pupils, as well as teaching farming and other useful occupations. The Church's orphanages and asylums provided a mother's care, one of the religion's finest features, and the sisters of Nazareth, who ran this home too gave themselves body and soul to the care of the orphan boys. However, Sid, as many before experienced hardship.

To enforce discipline the staff, carried leather straps. Misplacing her strap, one of the sisters on noticing Sid had not crossed himself when passing the statue of the Virgin Mary in the garden, picked up a stout wooden stick and struck him about his arm and shoulder. Sid though stunned and in pain, did not make a sound. Angered, the sister told him that after supper and prayers, he would go to the square at the back of the grounds, which was used as a boxing ring. On arriving Sid realised that he would be competing in the ring. His first opponent was a boy his own age and build, whom he beat easily. Another boy was brought forward, and again Sid won, following this, an older well-built boy came in to the ring, and Sid, being determined and stubborn, beat this boy too. By this time, although tired and bruised, Sid managed to hold his own against the sister's plan of humiliation.

After the boys in his dormitory were asleep, Sid crept out to the wash room to bathe his cuts and bruises. Returning but unable to sleep, Sid's mind drifted to thoughts of Virginia, wondering how she was, and if she was managing in Nazareth House. Virginia was small for her age and he knew she too would be missing their mother. Never having been apart before, he was concerned, having always looked after his younger sister and more so recently as she had started school in Coal Creek. This all seemed so far away, and Douglas, where was he? Wandering in and out of these thoughts Sid eventually drifted off to sleep, his hands, face and arms still throbbing.

Sid kept a low profile after the boxing experience, trying to keep out of harm's way. He prayed in chapel, hoping like Virginia that his mother would soon come for him. No-one questioned the fact that he was Anglican, but all the while he was being watched by one of the priests, his mop of thick, reddish blond hair standing out among the other boys. After prayers one evening, Father Joseph stopped Sid in the long corridor on his way back to the dormitory. The rest of the boys filed on, one or two nudging one another, giving knowing looks, but hurrying on their way and keeping their heads bowed.

Opening the door to his office Father Joseph pushed Sid into the dimly lit room with its small lamp on a corner table. The wood panelled walls were dark and dismal with one wall lined with books, the mullioned window on the wall opposite the door looked out to the gardens at the back, which were now dark, quiet and still. The Father's desk was large, dusty and covered with books, papers and a large Bible as he had been preparing the next day's morning Mass. The wooden chair behind his desk was low backed and slatted, with a dark, red leather seat edged with brass studs. Sid seeing the cane lying on the top of the papers, shivered, his mind racing, wondering what he could have done wrong in their eyes, nothing he could remember, or even imagine. The older man sat down. Telling Sid to come round and kneel down in front of him. He pulled him by his thick hair, closer between his open legs. He kept hold of Sid's hair while with his other hand the priest opened the buttons of his trousers bringing out his pulsating, glistening member. Sid struggled, trying to get to his feet but the harder he struggled the stronger the priest's hold and the stronger his desire. He pulled Sid's face over his throbbing penis and told him to suck him. He moved Sid's head back and forth, grunting and groaning with each movement till ejaculating in the boy's mouth. Sid choked and gagged. The priest pushed him to the floor, and grabbing the cane beat him till he collapsed and with his hands on the desk, gasping for breath. Moments later after kicking Sid like an animal, he told him to get out. He would be watching him, as he was now his special boy.

Stumbling to the door, Sid, spitting and wiping his mouth on his sleeve, while gasping for breath, ran to the washroom where he retched and retched till, he was sick. Splashing cold water on his face, rinsing out his mouth and spitting the vile fluids down the drain, he eventually gathered strength to head back to the dormitory. Clearing his mind would not be so easy. The dormitory was quiet and in spite of involuntary shivering he replaced his clothing with his nightshirt and slipped into bed covering himself with the rough blanket, and sobbed quietly. In a low whisper, John in the next bed leant over, asking if he was alright. Sid did not answer, he couldn't. Yet somehow, he knew John understood.

Sid decided there and then to run away, back to his father in Coal Creek Flats. He would stow away on the Christchurch-Greymouth express, the one he, Virginia and his mother had arrived on, but when that was, he couldn't remember.

CHAPTER 29
Kalimpong, India
1906

'Praise God from whom all mercies flow

On the 24th September 1900 the first children were admitted into the Homes, which was on land leased from the Government of Bengal. Soon Dr Graham would lease 100 acres and then over the years a total of 400 acres, as the Homes continued to grow. Soon to be established as a vocational training school, where the children would learn a trade, then be shipped to the British Colonies, of New Zealand, Australia and Canada to establish themselves using the job skills learnt in Kalimpong. The numbers of abandoned children were growing. The 'poor whites', unacknowledged mixed-race children of British fathers and native mothers. Children of British army personnel, administrators and tea planters, shunned by the British and upper-class Indians, most of the children would end up on city streets if it hadn't been for Dr Graham, wearing the hat of a social reformer, and finding a solution for this contemporary problem.

Each year the anniversary was celebrated. The staff had the usual programme of a service in the school, however, by 1906 the service was held in some comfort in the new Jarvie Hall, their hearts full of gratitude as they were able to meet as a large family, singing together *Let us with a gladsome mind, Praise the Lord for he is kind.* The hall was opened on 24th April 1906 by Sir L. Hare, officiating Lt. Governor of Bengal, and named after the late Major Jarvie of Bearsden, Glasgow, Scotland, whose legacy founded its construction. Tea and photographs always followed on this auspicious day and the stirring and much appreciated addresses were given by Mr James Luke of the Calcutta Committee and the Marine Society of India, along with two other Calcutta friends of the Home, a Mr. Thomson and a Mr. Le Patourel. The children sang, the younger ones with gusto some pretty little action songs, charming everyone, the celebration finishing with songs beautifully sung by Mrs Le Patourel.

A few older children, by this time, had moved on, some to British East Africa, some to Scotland, a few to the Royal Navy and others working on experimental farms for the Indian Government. Staff too had moved on, through ill health, or marriage. New cottages and additions to the school were being built, including the Georgina McRobert Memorial Tower, to house a clock with a chime of bells which would become the high centre of the children's village. The McRobert Tower, opened in June 1907, was named after the late wife of Mr A. McRobert, of Cawnpore, who had funded the tower and the chimes. The provision of donated money also enabled the building of the long wished for Hospital and Sanitorium, and the Steel Memorial which was opened on 4th February 1908 by Miss L. Steel, one of the donors, and named after Mr Octavious Steel of the Octavious Steel & Company, Calcutta. The construction was funded in memory of relations connected with India, joining the eight cottages, farm steading and workshops, school and play-shed. Although the Indian Government gave a capital grant, with 200 children by 1907, R100 a day was needed from public subscription to carry on the work.

The largest number of the children were still too young to start special training for their futures. The older ones however worked full or part time on the farm in the hope of going forward to the Provincial Agricultural College, with others working in the workshops, to a standard comparing favourably with apprentices elsewhere. Their first job was making furniture for the cottages, eventually saving the Homes money, and soon the boys gained enough experience to produce first class furniture to sell at the market in Kalimpong.

Science and Mathematics teachers had been added to the staff in the hope that some of the boys would go on to the Engineering College at Shibpur, to which the St Andrews School was now affiliated, or to the Arts College in Ranchi. It was cooler in Ranchi due to its altitude, picturesque too with many waterfalls and surrounding forests. Ranchi was considered a Hill Station, and Europeans flocked there in search of better health.

A Commercial Department for shorthand and typing was eventually introduced and Hindi classes as well. With the opening of the new hospital, selected girls began their training as nurses or mothers-helps, for which there was a great demand in the colonies. Life was busy and full for children and adults alike. Mrs Katherine Graham also encouraged the Kalimpong Home Industries, producing knitted goods, such as socks, vests and jumpers, and woven goods like Tibetan patterned cloths for purdah the female seclusion, and handmade lace, such as bridal veils, alter sets, fans, and lace trimmings and edging. This was not only for the older children to earn money for the Homes but to help educate the native hill women around Kalimpong.

The Inter-Cottage Garden Competition brought out the competitive spirit in everyone with the hard work resulting in some wonderful blooms around the cottages which were judged in late summer by Mr Thomson of the Government Cinchona Plantation in Munsong, West Bengal, a scenic hamlet adjacent to Kalimpong. Members of the Children's Special Services Mission also spent some weeks visiting the Homes, conducting Scripture Union Meetings along with the much anticipated and talked about evening lantern slide show in the School Hall. The group then visited the children in their individual cottages for talks and this was always greatly appreciated and enjoyed by the children and staff alike. The YMCA held socials in the Jarvie Hall and the Christian Endeavour Society also held hearty meetings, filling the young boys and girls with great hopes for their futures.

So, life in the Homes continued with constant movement and hopeful subscriptions.

CHAPTER 30
1912
Farewell India

Every year young men and women moved on from the Colonial Homes, to the far corners of the world.

> *Forget me not! Though far away*
> *You know that I love thee.*
> *Enshrined thou art within my breast*
> *Dear love, remember me.*
>
> *Anon*

In October 1912 the biggest farewell took place. A group of older boys and girls, young men and women really, sailed to New Zealand under the care of a Miss Mary Kennedy. They sailed on the British India Steam Navigation Co's *SS Sangola* to Melbourne and on to Dunedin on the *SS Warrimoo*. As most of these students had been at the Homes for over ten years, it was not only a great change for them but a financial loss for the Homes.

The party consisted of six girls including Dolly Higgins and seven boys. Travelling by train to Calcutta, part of the journey from Darjeeling on the Toy Train to Siliguri at the foot of the Himalayas, was for Dolly her last view of the great mountain range, which she had first seen as a small child back in 1897 and again with Maggie Leslie on their return to Calcutta from the Darjeeling sanitorium. So this was her final farewell to Northern India, her home for the last eleven years. She was now returning to Calcutta her first home. It was here in the Hall of the United

Free Church in Wellesley Street on the 23rd October 1912, that a large gathering of Friends of the Homes gave the young party a rousing send off. Mr R. H. A. Gresson, the Sheriff of Calcutta, presided over the delightful social gathering. In the beautifully decorated hall, where refreshments were served by the ladies of the congregation. The young emigrants being presented with a Bible and Hymn Book by the Bible Society's secretary, the Rev Mr Willifer Young. Praising the Kalimpong Homes for their great work, the Sheriff was glad to hear that they were growing steadily stronger, onward and upward, always expanding, and that funds were readily forthcoming for every good work undertaken. Only the other day he had read that Their Excellencies, Lord and Lady Carmichael, on a recent visit to the Homes, had opened a new road and several more buildings. Sheriff Gresson reported that the boys recently sent to a training ship in England were now serving in the merchant service. Unbeknown to everyone, the boys now serving in the merchant service, would soon be serving their new country in the First World War, many paying with their lives.

Recognition of the valuable training given in Kalimpong was even today spreading, and Sheriff Gresson wished the young migrants every success in their new life in New Zealand. The Church Hall in Wesley Street resounded with loud cheering. In response, the young group waved and shouted thank you, smiling and hugging one another. The main farewell party and the young migrants then happily joined the main body of church people and Kalimpong friends for the welcome tea and cakes. Such was the excitement of the young group, Dolly included, that not many realised that once they reached their final destination, most of them would be parted, never to meet again. The close knit, community life in Kalimpong, would be gone forever. Each would be on their own, in a strange land with little security and help. Little money too, something they had never needed before. Frugal though things had been, the youngsters were always provided for. This would certainly be a strange new experience for them.

The party being hailed a great success was carefully reported in the local press the following day, along with a charming photograph of the excited group. That same morning, the young migrants were joined on the quay side by many of the previous evenings farewell party, including their church sponsors who had given them a bed, for their last night in India. There were mixed emotions as the young people shook hands with their hosts, who wished them well in their new venture. The quayside was the usual hustle and bustle, smells and colours, that Dolly remembered from the day she and her father had met Aunt Dorothea on her arrival from England, nearly fifteen years before. As a tightness grasped Dolly's chest and tears stung her eyes, she remembered her tiny hand tightly clasping her father's, as they struggled through the crowds making their way to the gangway to meet Aunt Dorothea. How long ago it seemed, yet still clear in Dolly's mind's eye. Much had happened since that day, much of which she could never have imagined. Once again, the course of her life was being decided by others, as it had been previously by William and Dorothea. Dolly wondered where they were now after all these years, but doubted if they ever gave her a thought. She had never heard from them, or from her father. Had it all been a dream? Had it ever happened? Her little silver rattle safely tucked away in her bag the only proof that it had.

'Come on girls, come on Dolly, come on Margaret, pick up your bags, it's time we moved along, time to board the ship,' shouted Margaret's brother Robert Ochterloney one of the young men in their group. 'Bye', shouted Dolly to the farewell committee, her words lost in the melee as she and Margaret scrambled to pick up their bags and carefully mount the gangway, trying not to trip over the hems of their new white dresses. The other girls did the same, steadying themselves by the handrail, they climbed the gangway of the *SS Sangola*.

A new life was beginning.

CHAPTER 31

Aboard the British India Steam Ship *Sangola*
October 1912

An exile all in heart and frame
A wanderer weary of the way
A stranger without love's sweet claim
On any heart, go where you may.

Frances Sargent Osgood

The *SS Sangola* was built by William Denny & Bros on the River Clyde, Glasgow, Scotland, though their shipyard was actually on the river Leven, a tributary of the Clyde. A merchant ship launched in 1901 and owned by the British India Steam Navigation Company from 1901 – 1923, then sold on to Fukuhara Kisen and renamed the *Goshu Maru*, serving her Japanese owners till eventually being scrapped in 1933. From 1908 - 1910 the *SS Sangola* made six voyages to Fiji taking Indian indentured labourers from Calcutta and Madras. In 1912 the group of Kalimpong Orphan Eurasians too were taken to labour in the British colonies of Australia and New Zealand. Two years later, in 1914, she served as a troop ship, carrying Indian troops to Marseilles, France.

Sailing slowly out into the holy Hoogly River leaving behind one of Calcutta's busiest, noisiest and most colourful quays. The farewell party's exuberant cheering and waving soon melted into the daily hubbub of locals bathing, collecting water, washing clothes, with many performing their ritual cleansings at the Bathing Ghat. The river was the most westerly and commercially important arm of the Ganges. The broad steps or ghats, leading down to the water, a brilliant splash of colour with the moving milling throng of local people attending to their daily chores, heedless of the passengers watching attentively. Gazing over the side of the ship, Dolly and her friends were captivated by the scene, as the Hoogly river lazily meandered through the heart of Calcutta. The building of the recreational ghats, allowed people to appreciate the beauty of the Holy River. Armenians were among the earliest foreign immigrants to settle in Calcutta and the Armenian Ghat, was a large flower market displaying a remarkable variety of rare, and beautiful blooms. Lilies, Dutch Rose, Gladioli, Dahlias, were abundantly displayed in and around the market stalls. Dolly remembered seeing this many years ago when she visited with her mother and father. Her eyes grew moist as she gazed at the people toiling away at their daily chores. She realised soon this would be lost to her forever. One of the Kalimpong boys shouted, breaking the spell, calling to the girls to look over at the open-air wrestling. Several budding wrestlers competing against one another, their strong muscled bodies glistening in the sunshine, and being encouraged by their friends and local supporters cheering enthusiastically. Close by the riverside was a massage therapist, and at the edge of the ghat but further along, several boatmen were working and singing, preparing their boats for inviting trips along the river, to view the majestic temples and discover the charms of Calcutta, the City of Joy, which only the previous year, had become the capital of the Indian State of West Bengal.

Edging its way out of the city, the *Sangola* carried the young émigrés from security into an unknown world, far from the high protective Himalayas and the Silk Road which meandered passed Kalimpong on its way to the West. The merchant ship with its six cabins sailed on its way to the East, covering nearly 6,000 nautical miles to Melbourne, Australia. where the little party would then board the *SS Warrimoo* on to New Zealand. First however, there would be long days and nights at sea. Time for Dolly to reflect and contemplate, trying to imagine what life would be like in the new world. This was the last time Dolly, and many of her companions, would see the land of their birth.

Her friend, and now travelling companion, May Sinclair, from Lucia King Cottage had written in Dolly's diary a couple of days before their departure from the Homes;

> *If you have kind words to say*
> *Say them now.*
> *Tomorrow may not come your way,*
> *Give a kindness while you may,*
> *Hard ones will not always stay.*
> *Say them now.*
>
> *If you have a smile to show,*
> *Show it now*
> *Make hearts happy, roses grow,*
> *Let the friends around you know*
> *The love you have before they go*
> *Show it now.*

Anon

Dolly would treasured this all her life, along with other poems and thoughts from friends in Kalimpong, written with feeling before leaving, and with others added during the long voyage.

CHAPTER 32
The Long Sea Voyage
1912

So, the *Sangola* began its long sea voyage. Steaming out along the lower course of the Ganges-Brahmaputra basin where humid, tropical, deciduous forests, the natural habitat of the Bengal tiger, grow, and yielding valuable timber such as Sal, Teak and the large sacred evergreen Peepal, where Lord Brahma and Lord Vishnu live according to Hindu mythology. Sailing on out into the heat and humidity of the delta region, edged with mangrove trees which grow in saline coastal waters, forming a barrier against violent storm surges and floods, quite different from the high mountain regions and clear air to which Dolly and her companions were familiar. The world's largest delta, with its muddy waters emptying into the Bay of Bengal in the north eastern part of the Indian Ocean. To the west and northwest, India, and bounded on the north by Bangladesh, then on the east where they were now heading, Burma.

Calcutta to Rangoon being over 900 nautical miles would take the *Sangola* four days, time to acclimatise, as they neared the equator. The accommodation was cramped, but adequate and clean. Of the six passenger cabins, Miss Kennedy, their chaperone, occupied one. The girls shared two cabins as did the boys. The *Sangola*, though transporting immigrants, was a merchant ship, taking cargoes of tea and jute to Australia and New Zealand. The days at sea were long and hot, the nights equally long, hot and humid. Excitement gathered however, as the *Sangola* steamed steadily through the waters of the Bay of Bengal onward to Burma, and the port of Rangoon.

The Kalimpong party excited to be setting foot on land once more after their long days at sea, happily disembarked for an afternoon tour of the city, organised by the local Scots Kirk, to be followed by a reception at the manse.

CHAPTER 33

Christchurch
1938

Having settled Sid and Virginia in their respective Homes, Dolly made her way back to the Carlton Hotel to take up the promised post as a room maid. On arrival, Dolly let the receptionist and housekeeper know that her two children were now settled, for the time being, in the Nazareth House and St Joseph's Home. Then going up to her room, she sat for a few moments on the edge of the bed gathering her thoughts. Dolly had never been apart from Sid and Virginia, she felt sad and concerned. True Douglas was gone, yet never a day went by that she did not think or worry about him. Why had he left, disappearing so suddenly and on his birthday? Why had his step father Syd Stewart not stopped him?

Kathleen, her first born, would now be twenty-one, perhaps even married. Dolly understood she had gone to a good family in Christchurch, the Pauli's, known to the Ensors. Mrs Ensor having arranged for the adoption. She had been a lovely child, part Maori, from her father Lex Thorpe, who had died on the Western Front, in 1917. Kathleen now had a new name, and Dolly had heard she had moved to Australia following her adoptive parents' deaths. She had inherited their house next door to the house they had built for her. Not only had Kathleen a new surname, but she also changed her first name, making it now more difficult to trace her.

And Hector, where was he? Dolly had occasionally heard from 'the kind lady', Ethel, who had adopted him. They lived on a farm in the Golden Bay area, but had to move on when her husband James died back in 1930. Ethel had taken Hector to live with her son Colin, his wife and boys near Nelson, till she found somewhere new to live. Eventually moving to the Dovedale area near Motueka, where two of her daughters and their families lived. A sort of nomadic life, moving around, nowhere really to call their own, Dolly thought. Eventually, Hector however returned to live with Ethel in Dovedale. Her daughter Mavis Hawkes rented a little wooden house surrounded by fields, with chooks for eggs, and a milk cow. Hector went to Dovedale school with her son, his cousin Roddy, later continuing and finishing his education as a boarder at Nelson College. He started his training as a telegrapher at college, before then signing up to join the Royal New Zealand Navy and going on to serve in the Second World War with the British Royal Navy. Like Dolly as a child, surrounded by countryside and mountains, Hector lived in a rural part of the country under the watchful gaze of snow-capped Mount Arthur, rather than Mount Kanchenjunga, and in the distance the Richmond Range whose tops also glistened with snow through the winter months, though nothing like the heavy snow covering on the towering Himalayas.

So, Dolly's working life continued, dusting, cleaning and bedmaking, enjoying the conversation of the other women and learning about life in modern Christchurch. It had been many years, over twenty, since Dolly had first arrived in Christchurch from Dunedin back in 1917. Psregnant with her first daughter Kathleen, and alone.

During the few hours Dolly had off in the afternoons, she scanned the local press and shop windows for rooms to let, suitable for herself and the children. This was foremost in her mind, she had to be independent, financially too, and this was not easy. Then, sooner than anticipated Dolly had to move out of the Carlton, with spring approaching and business picking up, her room was needed for guests. However, with the help of one of the other domestics, Mary, who had a room in a nearby boarding house, Dolly moved in to a recently vacated upper room, in the same property. The room was close to work, affordable, but small, so no space for the children. It gave Dolly time however, to save and start looking in earnest for more suitable rooms.

Nearly six months would pass before Dolly was in a position to collect the children from the Homes to join her in the two roomed rented flat above a baker's shop, fortunately not far from the hotel and the local school.

CHAPTER 34

Christchurch – Deliverance
1938

With visits to St Joseph's Home and Nazareth House not actually encouraged, and as most of the children were either abandoned or orphaned, having a mother visit regularly was not something the priests and sisters were used to, or even happy about. Dolly however persevered, eventually being told that Sid was no longer in St Joseph's.

'Disappeared without trace, a troubled boy', they alleged.

'No, he had not asked for his mother, he just ran away, not unusual, many boys do.' As Dolly had put him into the Home, they guessed she had wanted rid of him, so no one had bothered trying to contact her.

Gasping, and choking for breath, Dolly fled out of St Joseph's, crying and stumbling, unable to believe what she had been told. How could this possibly have happened? No feasible explanation, just that he seemed troubled, but why troubled?

In spite of her eyes brimming with tears, feeling traumatised and confused, Dolly somehow managed to find her way to Nazareth House, ignoring the strange looks from passersby. All she wanted was her daughter. Ringing the bell and banging on the door, for what seemed ages, till one of the sisters eventually answered and opened the door. Dolly, pushing passed her, ran into the main hall, shouting Virginia's name at the top of her voice. Almost immediately doors began opening around the hall and on the upper balcony. Sisters appeared, closely followed by young girls all talking at once, wondering what the shouting and screaming was about, a good excuse though to get out of the classroom. One of the older sisters, cautiously approached Dolly trying to calm her down, asking her quietly what was wrong. Dolly managed to gasp out Virginia's name, saying she wanted to see her daughter immediately.

Slowly, from behind a small group of girls across the Main Hall, Virginia appeared. Nervously walking over to where Dolly stood, she held out her trembling hands, 'Mummy', she said, 'I am here, I want to come home, I have missed you so much.' Dolly's already tear-filled eyes slowly focused on her young daughter. Hesitantly taking a few steps forward, she encircled Virginia in her arms, holding her close. Never in Dolly's life had anyone ever missed or wanted her - not since her own mother, who had died over forty years before in Darjeeling, and her father who had disappeared during the Assam earthquake of 1897 - as she wanted her child now. The years of loneliness and abandonment suddenly overcame her in a fierce mixture of love and pain, leaving those looking on bewildered. Dolly knelt down, gazing into her weeping daughter's tear-stained face, stroking her dark hair, and speaking softly to her. She had noticed that Virginia's knees and shins were red and sore, her little hands too, which she now held and kissed. Dolly stood up, slowly looking round at the whispering, nudging crowd, then gently taking Virginia's hand, and with new found mental and physical strength, walked quickly to the main door. Never glancing back. Mother and daughter descended the stone steps out into the sunshine with Dolly silently thanking God, if there was one, for deliverance.

CHAPTER 35
Rangoon - Burma
October 1912

A thriving mercantile capital, and as important as Calcutta, Rangoon or Yangon was founded as Dagon in the early 11th century, by the Mon people of Lower Burma, and subsequently captured by the British in the second Anglo- Burmese War of 1852, transforming it into a commercial and political hub. Based on designs by army engineer, Lt. Alexander Fraser, the British constructed a new city on the delta at the confluence of the Pegu and Myitmaka rivers, emptying into the Gulf of Martaban in the Andaman Sea. Rangoon became the capital of all British–ruled Burma after capturing Upper Burma in 1885. Increasing commerce and population brought prosperous residential suburbs, with an increasing need for hospitals and colleges. With its spacious parks and lakes, mix of modern buildings and traditional wooden architecture, Rangoon became the 'Garden of the East'. Indeed, by the early 20th century, it's public services and infrastructure put it on a par with London.

Many of the down town buildings were English in style, but were more accurately a sample of Scottish architectural influence. Thousands of Scots had lived and worked in the city, and may have constituted as much as 80% of the European population in colonial times. The majority of top companies in Rangoon in the late 19th century and early 20th century were Scottish. - the Irrawaddy Flotilla Company, Grindlays Bank, Burma Oil and Bombay Burma, were all Glasgow registered companies. Scotland had deep ties with Burma, and so it was that the Presbyterian Church known as the Scots Kirk in Rangoon, was pleased to welcome the Kalimpong migrants to their city. The ladies of the Kirk planned a welcoming tea with an enticing spread of sandwiches and rich and colourful cakes, with decorative dishes laden with colourful fresh fruit. Dr Graham's 'Begging Bowl' reached far and wide, so the Scots Kirk and the Rev James A Drysdale and his flock, felt they were welcoming their own.

A tour of the city had been organised. Rangoon was an enticing and colourful spread of not only the West but of the East, with wonderful golden pagodas, sparkling and shining in the bright sunlight. Having been met at the dockside by the Kirk's 'welcoming committee' arriving with a small convoy of charabancs, the young travellers were taken to the Cantonment Gardens, situated south west of the Shwe Dagon Pagoda within the military cantonment. Standing over 300ft high, the 14th century Pagoda, was also known as the Golden Pagoda, containing four relics of previous incarnations of the Buddha and was Burma's most important Buddhist temple.

The gardens, planned around 1855 by William Scott of the Calcutta Botanic Gardens,
were centred to look upon the gold plated, diamond studded spire of the pagoda. Shimmering against the skyline and reflecting in the sparkling lake, the view took the groups breath away. Crossing the rustic bridge to the summerhouse Miss Kennedy and the party sat for a while admiring the gilded, bell shaped stuppa, which could be seen from all over Rangoon, due to its elevated position on Sung Uttara Hill. It was wonderful to feel solid ground beneath their feet again and to enjoy the colourful sights, sounds and tempting aromas of Rangoon, rather than gazing out at endless sea, and having previously only glimpsed at in books back in the Homes, the world was now opening up before them, stimulating feelings of wonder and excitement, before unknown.

The afternoon tea at the Scots Kirk was a welcome respite from hopping off and on the charabancs. Taking in all the sites and listening to the historic musings of their knowledgeable hosts had been interesting, but a lot to take in, making the afternoon tea even more welcome. The girls enjoyed listening to the ladies of the Kirk talk about life in Rangoon and happily answered their questions about the Homes, especially what it was like living in isolation on top of the world. The Kirk donated money to the Homes and kept in touch with Dr Graham, so now this gave a personal meaning to their giving.

The Rev Drysdale, knighted some years later, rounded off the joyful gathering with an encouraging speech, sending the Kalimpong group off with resounding encouragement, hoping they would not forget their visit to Rangoon. Perhaps if time and memory allowed, to occasionally keep in touch, once they had settled in to their new life in New Zealand. Tired but happy, Dolly and her group were taken back to the docks to board the *Sangola*, in time to catch the evening tide. No one seemed hungry, not even the boys, so soon after their memorable spread, and were content to go to their cabins and rest. Soon the *Sangola* was slipping out of the Port of Rangoon on the next part of the journey. The young migrants went back up on deck to catch a final glimpse of the Golden Pagoda sparkling in the pink evening light. This mystical view left a lasting memory in Dolly's mind.

Out into the Gulf of Martaban and on into the Andaman Sea, through the Straits of Malacca and on to the Island of Penang and George Town, Malaya. Each with their own memories of their day in Rangoon, and possibly wondering if they would ever return.

> *When the golden sun is setting,*
> *When from care your heart is free,*
> *When of others you are thinking,*
> *Will you sometimes think of me?*
>
> Bobby Newcombe, 1877

Returning to their cabins the group including Miss Kennedy slept soundly.

> *Go! Sleep like closing flowers at night*
> *And Heaven thy morn will bless.*
>
> Henry T. Coates

The first stop on their long journey, Rangoon, was hailed a success, and in four days' time their next stop Penang would open up to them. Warmer too, as they neared the equator, with virtual endless summer. Quite different from the five seasons they were used to in Kalimpong. Spring, summer, autumn, winter and the monsoons.

CHAPTER 36

Penang – The Pearl of the Orient
1912

Captain Francis Light, the founder of Penang, named Prince of Wales Island in honour of the Prince of Wales, George, later King George 1V. A town was established, and named George Town, also after the prince. The captain landed in August 1786 on the island of Penang, originally part of the Malay Sultanate of Kedah. Persuading the Sultan to relinquish Penang to the Honourable East India Company Service, in exchange for protection against the Burmese and Siamese armies, Francis Light established Penang as the first British trading post in the Far East, flourishing as a port of call for shipping on the India-China run. In the end no protection was given, fighting ensued, and the Sultan was defeated. The skirmishes settled, and still today over two hundred years later, the Penang State Government pays 18,000,000 Malaysian Ringgit (MYR) annually to the Sultan of Kedah, over £3,000,000.

Penang became a crossroads of great civilizations, a melting pot of traders and settlers from Europe, India, China, the Malay Archipelago, Thailand and Burma. From 1826 till 1867 it was part of the Straits Settlement under the British Administration, then under direct British Colonial rule till war broke out in December 1941. The Japanese invaded Malaya, bombing Penang, the British fleeing to Singapore. From 1942 till the Japanese surrender in 1945, Penangites lived in fear of torture and death at the hands of the invaders.

As in Rangoon, there was a strong Scottish connection in Penang, with streets and buildings named after famous Scots. The most famous street being Jalan Scotland, mostly referred to as Scotland Road. Others being McNair Street, Logan Road, Campbell Street and McAlister Road. Four sons of the Scottish family McAlister of the clan McAlister from Scotland's North West coast, served with the East India Company. Colonel Norman McAlister of the Bengal Army was sworn in as Lieutenant-Governor of Penang in 1807. Colonel McAlister was a friend and associate of Sir Stamford Raffles who founded the British Colony of Singapore in 1819, and in 1839 it replaced Prince Edward Island as the principal British naval port in Asia. Sadly, Colonel McAlister was drowned at sea while returning to Scotland in 1810 on the East Indiaman *Ocean*.

Along Northam Road in Penang the previous Dutch Reformist Church was taken over by the Scottish Presbyterian community in the early 19th century. Now named St Andrew's Church or the Scots Kirk. Opposite the parliament building, it has an arched pediment roof, twin towers, a projecting porch, and a rusticated colonnade at the side. The Kirk, built of brick, lime and timber, and surrounded by a garden of palm trees, is one of the oldest remaining buildings in Penang. The new minister of the Scots Kirk William Cross, and the congregation were delighted to be entertaining the young Kalimpong students, as the congregation financially supported Dr Graham and the St Andrew's Homes.

Quite early after a basic breakfast and freshen up, the little party gathered on deck to watch the *Sangola* dock. Around and along this part of the large sprawling harbour, large colonial buildings edged the busy road, which ran along by the side of the water. Many of the buildings were headquarters of the commercial trades being plied back and forth across the deep strait. There was great excitement as they watched the comings and goings. The harbour was noisy and busy with other steam ships arriving and departing. Careful negotiations were needed to avoid collision with the many colourful Chinese sampans and junks plying back and forth across the channel.

The early lucrative trade of Penang was tea, spices, especially clove and nutmeg from local farms, black pepper from Banda Acheh, textiles from India, and later rubber and tin. A massive boom in the rubber trade came in the first decade of the 20th century, as prices rose and global demand grew, with rubber plantations spreading across the Malay peninsula. In front of their eyes, the geography lessons, which Dolly and the group had learnt about in school were unfolding. It was so much to take in, unbelievable really.

Soon the group were ushered by Miss Kennedy towards the gangway and down to meet the awaiting party. The girls wore the cool, white dresses, which they had shortened during the voyage, not only allowing more freedom of movement, but were cooler. Their wide brimmed hats protected them from the persistent sun. The boys also wore hats, white shirts and loose cotton trousers, similar to their Kalimpong uniform. Once again charabancs were at the dock side, with their chaperones from the Scots Kirk coming to greet them. Welcomes and introductions over, everyone piled in and sat down, chatting excitedly, ready to enjoy their guided tour of George Town.

Like Rangoon, George Town was a colourful, multicultural capital overlooked by Penang Hill, a mountainous park. Ornate Chinese temples, Hindu temples and the Kek Lok Si Buddhist Temple, each a wonderful, colourful work of art, lining their route. Passing markets and street traders, busy local people carrying on with their daily lives, occasionally smiling at the young group passing through this magical tableau. Eventually the charabancs arrived the Penang Botanical Gardens or 'Waterfall Gardens', where they stopped to have the welcome picnic. The gardens were established in 1884, out of an old quarry surrounded by an amphitheatre of hills, by the superintendent of the Singapore Botanic Gardens,

Nathaniel Cantley and his assistant Charles Curtis. Despite a threat to turn the valley where the gardens were located back into a reservoir, the natural lush greenery of the tropical rain-forest was a tranquil setting under the shade of the trees, making an ideal place for a picnic.

Not alone, the group had to watch out for dusky leaf monkeys found in the Malayan peninsular, short-tailed Asian macaques, as well as many large, never before seen insects, and beautifully, coloured butterflies. Settling down on the tartan rugs provided by their hosts, everyone was soon chatting enthusiastically about all they had seen. Enjoying the sandwiches and drinking the fresh lemonade provided by the ladies of the Kirk. Questioning their hosts about life in Penang, the Kennedy group then delighted their guides with tales of Kalimpong. The students were reminded of the many picnics held in the surrounding hills and grounds of the cottages, the games they played, and happily regaled these memories, much to the delight of their chaperones.

Soon on their way again, heading back to the Scots Kirk, meeting up this time in the church hall, cheerfully decorated by the ladies of the congregation. Along with other church members, they were welcomed formally by the Minister, William Cross and the Kirk session. He was conscious of the St Andrew's Church connection to the St Andrew's Colonial Homes in Kalimpong. Also supporting the YMCA and starting the *St Andrew's Outlook* magazine developed from the congregation's Penang Journal he encouraged the young visitors to each take a copy of the *St Andrew's Outlook* with them to their new lives in New Zealand. It would remind them of their connection with *St Andrew* in Kalimpong, Penang and Scotland.

Only Dolly remembered the other St Andrews, the church in Darjeeling, with the old Christian graveyard, where her mother and grandmother lay buried amongst the first settlers and missionaries. Her daydream was abruptly interrupted with the sudden awareness of what was going on around her. Great cheering, not only for the Minister's inspiring words, but the arrival of the long-awaited spread of delicious afternoon tea, sandwiches and cakes. Listening too to many tales of life on the Peninsula by the exiled Scots, Miss Kennedy's group eventually and reluctantly gathered themselves together, thanking everyone for their kindness, and assuring them they would always remember their wonderful reception and exciting time in Penang.

Back onboard the *Sangola* some tears were shed by a few of the girls, sad that they were leaving this magical place, leaving behind kind people, and gloomy at the thought of the long days at sea before reaching Melbourne, Australia.

Forget me not though far away
You know that I love thee
Enshrined thou art within my breast
Dear love, remember me.

My thoughts are ever full of thee
I see thee in my dreams,
Light of my life, my star of hope
Whose radiance ever beams.

May Heaven bless thee, dearest one,
In thy home across the sea,
I hope to join thee soon my love,
Then we shall happy be.

Dolly's Me

Chapter 37

Christchurch, New Zealand
1938

Dolly was both relieved and pleased to have Virginia back with her again, as was young Virginia to be back with her mother, safely away from the gruesome experience of Nazareth House. The most important thing now was to get Virginia into school and be among children her own age. Hopefully helping to put the traumatic incidents of recent months to the back of her mind. The nearest school to where they lived was an Anglican Church School for boys and girls. So, taking a few hours off work, Dolly arranged Virginia's admission to the school and soon she was happily getting to know her new teacher, new classmates and making friends. She still missed her brother Syd, and in quiet moments often wondering where he was. Dolly never spoke of him, though Virginia was sure she must miss him too, he was her son.

So much had happened in the year since the little family had left Coal Creek Flats with 10/- their mother's pocket. Sid now gone, maybe even back to his father's farm. Douglas had disappeared; he would now be 17, and Hector 14, both growing up fast. Perhaps in the Nelson region, though Dolly wasn't sure as Hector and his grandmother Ethel seemed to move around, making any contact difficult. She knew that his grandfather James Crichton, Ethel's second husband, had died in the winter of 1930 when Hector was six. He and his adoptive mother Ethel, who had been previously married to an Ernest Bateman in 1889, had left the rented farm at Golden Bay and moved in with her daughter Mavis who lived in a little wooden house in Dovedale. Hector and his cousin Rodger, attended Dovedale Primary School and enjoyed playing for hours in the fields, climbing trees and guddling for fish in the streams. This love of the outdoors stayed with Hector all his life. Moving on to Nelson Boys College with his half-brother Robert, Colin's son, he excelled in sports. His future however, lay with the New Zealand Royal Navy, sailing off to war in 1941.

Settling in at school and making new friends Virginia also looked forward to home time and being back with her mother. On the days Dolly met her from school they enjoyed walking by the river Avon, or wandering round the local shops and buying something for their evening meal. Dolly managed to fit her work at the Carlton Hotel around Virginia's school hours, though sometimes having to go home from school by herself if the hotel was busy, and although missing her mother, she was a careful young girl, doing her homework then playing with her doll or reading till Dolly came home. Missing life on the farm at Coal Creek Flat she found city life confining and not very friendly. She missed the animals, the freedom to run across the paddocks and visiting Mrs Williams, who always had a bowl of soup and a piece of cake for Sid and herself, when she saw them passing on their way home from school.

Both Virginia and Dolly found this new life quite different, realising it would take some time to settle in.

CHAPTER 38
Long Sea Voyage to Melbourne
1912

Sailing again into the Strait of Malacca out of Penang, then north into the Andaman Sea, round the northern tip of Sumatra at Banda Aceh where the black pepper comes from, and on out into the Indian Ocean. Continuing south, leaving the Northern Hemisphere as they crossed the Equator, sailing on passed Christmas Island, and down along the West Coast of Australia. Crossing the Tropic of Capricorn and on into the Great Australian Bight, to the Bass Strait, then into the large basin of Port Phillip Bay, they arrived on the 6th December 1912 at Princes Pier, Port Melbourne at the mouth of the Yarra River, in the heat of high summer.

Contracted to land at Melbourne in the State of Victoria, the Kennedy group were again met by session members, this time of the Melbourne Scots Kirk, located on Collins Street. The building was designed to be *the most beautiful building in Australia* with construction starting in 1871 and opening on 29th November 1874, with fixed seating for around 1,000 people. The spire, at just over 200 feet high was the tallest structure in Melbourne. The church in Neo-Gothic style was designed by Joseph Reed and built by David Mitchell, the father of the celebrated opera singer Dame Nellie Melba.

The Victorian gold rush of the 1850s led to Melbourne rapidly developing from a scattering of wooden houses into a marvellous modern city. It was during this period that Reed and Mitchell

designed and built many imposing buildings, including the Royal Exhibition Centre. The Centre had housed in October 1880, The Melbourne International Exhibition, the first official World's Fair in the Southern Hemisphere.
Queen Victoria even appointed a Commision to promote the success of the exhibition and lent some of her paintings and allowed reproductions of some objects of regalia from the Tower of London to be sent and exhibited. It was certainly the greatest show the city had ever seen, and was repeated eight years later. The State Library, the Melbourne Town Hall and the imposing red brick built Sacred Heart Church, also designed by Joseph Reed, being one of the finest Baroque churches in the State. All quite different from the glistening golden pagodas of Rangoon, the exotic Chinese temples of Penang and even the great Victorian buildings in Calcutta, equally spectacular and wonderful to behold. Rightly too the congregation was proud of its Scots Kirk, with its impressive collection of large and small Christian themed stained-glass windows, basalt columns, timber beamed roof and elevated floor, allowing all a clear view of the pulpit.

Dolly and the group along with Miss Kennedy were escorted into the church building and settled in pews near the front. Being Advent and summer, the church was colourfully decorated with red and white poinsettias, and other exotic flowers giving off mysterious and sensory aromas. Quite a crowd had gathered. Seeming more than half full, with members of the congregation curious to meet the young migrants, on their last port of call on their journey to New Zealand.

Staying with members of the congregation till their date of departure, five days later, on 11th December 1912, the group were excited to see this amazing city. Later they would be boarding the *SS Warrimoo* for New Zealand via Hobart and contracted to land at Dunedin. Their old friend the *SS Sangola* and her crew were heading for Sydney on 12th December, taking two of the party from India and new passengers.

Their stay in Melbourne was a welcome change from nearly three weeks on the high seas. This was a modern, westernised city, something the group had never before experienced. English was spoken, but with quite a different accent. Excitedly the girls spent time looking in the shop windows, and wandering round the many department stores, gazing in amazement at all the goods that were for sale. Quite unlike the now distant bazaar which used to excite the youngsters on their walking trips in to Kalimpong.
Stopping for tea at the many street cafes was a luxury new to the group, such a different way of life, with Miss Kennedy exhausted trying to keep up with her charges. The congregation also organised tours around the city visiting the Exhibition Centre, the Royal Botanic Gardens with its mix of native and exotic plants, and a sightseeing cruise on the Yarra River between the Docklands and Williamstown. Far more exciting was the afternoon spent looking round the soon to be opened Luna Amusement Park which would go on to be a great success, with live performances at the Palace of Illusions and a permanent high-wire act. There was a Big Dipper roller coaster, a Noah's Ark, a Water Chute and a 4-row Carousel.

On the evening before their departure, they attended a farewell supper organised by the congregation in the church hall. The large hall was crowded with well-wishers, the tables groaning with sandwiches, fruit and fresh juice and doubtless beers for the men. Again a few tears were shed after the rousing speeches of goodwill and Godspeed, and an unexpected welcome cable from Dr Graham himself was read out, saying how proud he was of his students. Wishing them well he hoped to meet up with them again someday, when he himself would visit New Zealand.
Arriving back at the dock and with a farewell wave, the group boarded the *Warrimoo*. Settling into new cabins and hopefully getting some sleep, in spite of all the chatter and excitement, before they set sail the next morning on the final leg of their

journey to New Zealand.

New Zealand their new homeland, and for Miss Kennedy, the eagerness of returning home after five years of service as a house mother in Kalimpong. What awaited them they didn't know, but they were hopeful and everyone they had met so far on their journey had been welcoming, hospitable, encouraging, kind, and full of Christian blessings, as they waved them on their way, with Melbourne being no different.

> *Meeting is a pleasure*
> *Parting is a pain*
> *God be with you dear Dorothea*
> *Till we meet again.*

Anon

CHAPTER 39

The *SS Warrimoo*
1892 – 1918

Launched in May 1892 the *SS Warrimoo* was built by Swan Hunter of Wallsend on the River Tyne, Northumberland, for James Huddart's planned Trans-Tasman passenger service between Australia and New Zealand. However, the lucrative subsidies for carrying mail attracted him to provide a service between Sydney, Australia, and Vancouver, Canada. Huddart ran into financial difficulties after arranging to also call into New Zealand. The *Warrimoo* was then purchased by the New Zealand Shipping Company being further sold on in August 1899 to the Union Steamship Company of New Zealand Ltd. It was during this time at the turn of the century that the *Warrimoo* made notable history. Allegedly arriving at the crossing of the International Date Line and the Equator at midnight on 31st December 1899 under the captaincy of a John Phillips.

On its way from Vancouver to Australia knifing its way through the waters of the Mid-Pacific with the navigator working out a star fix, the captain realised the *Warrimoo's* position was latitude 0 degrees x 31 minutes north and longitude 179 degrees x 30 minutes west. The date was 31st December 1899 meaning they were only a few miles from the intersection of the Equator and the International Date Line. Taking full advantage of the opportunity to achieve the navigational freak of a lifetime, Captain Phillips called his navigator to the bridge to double check the ship's position. Changing course slightly and adjusting the engine speed, along with calm weather and a clear night working in their favour, at midnight the *Warrimoo* lay on the equator at the exact point where it crossed the International Date Line. The significances of this bizarre position were many. The forward part of the ship was in the Southern Hemisphere, in mid-summer on 1st January 1900 whilst the stern was in the Northern Hemisphere in mid-winter on 31st December 1899. For those few seconds the *Warrimoo* was in two different hemispheres, two different days, two different months, two different seasons and not only two different years but two different centuries, all at the same time.

Two years after the Kalimpong group set sail from Melbourne to New Zealand, in 1914 the *Warrimoo* was given the role of troop ship delivering the first Maori Pioneer military troops to *Galipoli* in 1915. In 1916 it was sold on again this time to Tan Kah Kee, also known as Chen Jiageng, who had four wives and seventeen children. He was a Chinese businessman, community leader, communist and philanthropist active in South East Asia. The ship then became part of the Khiam Yik company, a business empire based on rubber. In May 1918, before the end of the war, as part of a convoy from Bizerte, Tunisia, to Marseille the *Warrimoo* collided with the French warship *Catapult*, dislodging the warship's depth charges, which detonated. The resulting explosions ruptured the hulls of both vessels, resulting in the loss of lives and the loss of both ships.

CHAPTER 40
Christchurch, New Zealand
The War Years

The Second World War, the world's most destructive conflict, took the lives of up to 50 million people, of which 12,000 were New Zealanders. This may not seem many in comparison, but the population at that time was under two million. New Zealand had already lost over 16,000 killed, and over 41,000 wounded, in the First World War. So, although the Second World War was again being fought thousands of miles away in Europe, it was also being fought in the Pacific closer to home, and this was being felt in the hearts and minds of thousands back home in New Zealand. One of Dolly's sons Hector was serving with the RNZN, leaving from Lyttleton Harbour on the Banks Peninsula, South Island, Doug in the Expeditionary Force, so both fighting for King and Country, and would hopefully come home safely.

Hector, Dolly's third child was soon to experience his first taste of conflict at Guadalcanal. The Japanese had amassed a vast new defensive empire from Alaska in the north to the Solomon Islands in the South Pacific. The Pacific conflict fought on a vast scale over huge distances, was sparked by the Imperial Japanese Navy Air Service bombing the United States naval base at Pearl Harbour in Honolulu, Hawaii, just before 08.00hrs on Sunday morning, 7th December 1941.

The United States Marine Corps needed a base, so mounted its first amphibious landing of World War 11 at Guadalcanal, the principal island on the Province of the Solomon Islands. *Operation*

Watchtower, codenamed by the Corps, and fought between August 1942 and February 1943, was not only up against air bombardment by the Japanese, but strikes at New Zealand docks from where much of their supplies were coming. The trade unions were using the war as leverage for pay rise demands.

On 5th January 1943 the *HMS Achilles* was 'caught napping', as Hector later related, by four Japanese aircraft, and bombed. The gun turret was blown off and thirteen sailors killed. Hector's young friend died beside him, so escaping with his life he felt from that moment he would come through the war unscathed and his fear left him.

Between April 1943 and May 1944, the *Achilles* was docked in Portsmouth, England, for repairs. It was during this stay that the German Luftwaffe bombed Portsmouth to finish off the *Achilles* which had been at the scuttling and demise of the pocket battleship, the German Cruiser *Admiral Graf Spee* at the Battle of the River Plate. Unlike Portsmouth, the *Achilles* in dry dock, escaped unscathed. It was eventually sent back to the Royal New Zealand Naval fleet, joining the British fleet in May 1945 for the final operations in the Pacific.

Dolly and Virginia continued their life in Christchurch during this wartime period as best they could. Aware, like all New Zealanders, of the country's vulnerability as Japan attacked and conquered much of the area north of New Zealand and with submarine-launched Japanese float planes overflying Auckland and Wellington, no one felt really safe. New Zealand introduced rationing at this time largely to create a surplus of food to be used to feed the British and American allies. The American forces in the Pacific putting a strain on the New Zealand vegetable supply, eating around 137,000 tons during their four years in the Pacific. Rationing eventually ended in June 1952.

Back in September 1940, a year after the war had started, a

maintenance court order was made in favour of Doreen Ethel Stewart (Dolly) for £2 15/- prior to rationing, so this extra money had helped, adding to her wage at the Carlton Hotel. During this period of war time upheaval, Virginia was settling down and enjoying school with her young friends, and apart from reading, writing and arithmetic, Virginia was also learning to knit and sew, which she enjoyed in the evenings under Dolly's watchful eye, the wireless playing quietly in the background.

Christchurch, a handsome city, with many fine buildings, including the magnificent Gothic Revival Cathedral, named the Christ Church Catherdral, built between 1864 and 1904, and set in the heart of the city surrounded by Cathedral Square, was one of the places Dolly and Virginia liked to visit. It brought back memories of the Cathedral in Melbourne, some twenty eight years before. They also enjoyed walking by the side of the River Avon which edged the large and beautiful Botanic Garden, with its wide variety of displays, from English rose gardens to New Zealand ferns. The gardens, beautifully maintained, may not have been as exotic as the gardens Dolly remembered in Rangoon, but beautiful in their own right, and at least changing with the seasons. Dolly's favourite time was spring, when the flower beds were filled with large, golden headed daffodils dancing in the breeze, reflecting the colour of the warming sun, and deep purple iris, along the river bank. Closely followed by tulips, rich jewels of every hue.

During these wartime days, when walking in the gardens after work, passing time till meeting Virginia from school, and reflecting on her life during the last war, that Dolly, now in her late forties, met a Mr Smith, Alex. He was pleasant, interesting, and it turned out, lived not far from them. Petite as her name suggested, still pretty, and with her thick, dark wavy hair now heavily sprinkled with silver, she kept it short and bouncy. Long gone the thick dark plait she wore in Kalimpong and longer ago in Calcutta, in the days when her mother Margaret, brushed it every night before bedtime. All so long ago.

Alex walked the gardens most days around the same time as Dolly, and weather permitting, they often sat on one of the benches catching up with the daily news, mainly about the war, which was of course on the forefront of everyone's mind.
The daily rationing and family anxieties concerning loved ones overseas, and like everyone else, New Zealanders too longed for peace, but it would still be many long years in coming. Alex recalled his World War One service in German Samoa, reminding Dolly of Hector's grandfather, who had also been on the island during the conflict, though she never mentioned it.

One piece of encouraging news Dolly did receive in April 1942 was when a copy of the *Nelson Evening Mail* of the 15th, arrived from Ethel H Crichton of Motueka, as Dolly still occasionally kept in touch. Cabled news has been received by Mrs E H Crichton from her 'son' – telegraphist Hector F Crichton Royal New Zealand Navy stating that he is safe and well. Good news indeed which Dolly shared with Virginia, and for a while this brightened their lives, especially after having heard in February 1942, that her application to the magistrate court to increase the amount of maintenance to £3.10/- had been revoked, after an appeal by Sidney Stewart. The following year in April 1943 Dolly received notice of her divorce from Sidney Stewart, Coal Creek Flats. Having not given Sidney much thought, especially after the disappointment of the maintenance refusal, the previous February, she was surprised at the stomach-turning feeling, but soon realising it released her from that period of her life, allowing her to move on with her own future, whatever it might be.

Being now divorced, allowed Dolly to be more relaxed in Alex's company, and their friendship eventually became more serious. Dolly occasionally invited him round for afternoon tea and to meet Virginia. He was always polite, bringing Virginia little gifts of fruit or sweets. Being unused to adult male company, ten-year-old Virginia felt uncomfortable when he visited, was never really happy in his company. Avoiding eye contact and never saying much, which was unlike her, Dolly asked Virginia what was wrong, but not knowing how to explain to her mother her feelings, she said nothing.

CHAPTER 41

Christchurch
An End and a Beginning

In the *Nelson Evening Mail* of 19th October 1944, Ethel Crichton read another surprising and welcome cabled news advising that her *'son'* Hector, now a Leading Telegraphist on overseas service, *'is fit and well'*. Dolly felt reassured when she received a copy of the newspaper from Ethel, that at least one of her sons, all being well, would hopefully return home safely. No indication in the short brief that he was soon to become a father, on the other side of the world. In January 1945 Dolly's granddaughter was born in Northumberland, England, while her son's submarine was beneath the North Sea searching for German (Kriegsmarine) U-boats along the Norwegian coast, into the fjords and on up to the Arctic. With the overwhelming Allied efforts, Germany had lost over 120 U-Boats during the first five months of 1945, the war was reaching an end.

In May 1945, cabled news reached New Zealand welcoming the coming of peace in Europe, followed in August with victory over Japan. There was understandable relief, enthusiasm and feelings of jubilation, followed by celebration. Germany surrendered in the early afternoon of 7th May 1945, New Zealand time, and the news became known the next morning with huge headlines in the papers. However, the acting Prime Minister Walter Nash insisted that celebrations should wait until the British Prime Minister, Winston Churchill, officially announced peace.

The announcement came at 1.00am New Zealand time on the 9th May. So, celebrations for VE Day, 8th May, were held instead on the 9th and people went to work as usual on the 8th as advised over the wireless by the acting Prime Minister. The next day, Town Hall bells were ringing and flags raised. Speeches were made in the Government Buildings in Wellington, by the Governor General, the acting Prime Minister Walter Nash and the Opposition leader Sidney Holland. The National Anthems of America, Soviet Russia and New Zealand were played and sung, and only then and after midday did official local ceremonies begin. The celebrations extending over into the next day, which had also declared a public holiday.

There were marching bands, along with community singing. Thanks Giving Services were held at local war memorials, bonfires were lit, sports were organised for children and victory parties for the grown-ups. In Christchurch the Trades Council organised a People's Victory March with 26,000 people parading from Latimer Square to Cathedral Square, singing patriotic songs and waving flags. Dolly with Alex Smith and Virginia, who had a school holiday, joined in the parade, enjoying every minute of the excitement and friendship, with strangers hugging and kissing one another. People flung confetti and paper streamers out of windows, pubs were full, yet nothing got out of hand. In Cathedral Square Alex Smith proposed to Dolly, and in the overwhelming emotion of the moment she accepted.

The excitement of May carried into June and July and on into August, the winter months into early spring, and on the 15th August news of the Japanese surrender arrived at 11.00am. Again, with sirens sounding and bells ringing, a national ceremony was held and once more local celebrations were underway. There were parades, bonfires, bands, dancing and sports, and the beer continued to flow. Three days after the VJ Day celebrations in

August 1945 Alex and Dolly married, carried along in the great feelings of world celebration and freedom from tyranny.

Unbeknown to Dolly however, her tyranny was just beginning. Dolly Higgins, who had been Doreen Ethel Stewart, now became Doris Ethel Smith

CHAPTER 42
Arrival in Dunedin
1912

Originally to be called New Edinburgh, instead the township was called Dunedin, from the Gaelic *Dun Eideann*, or Edinburgh, Scotland's capital city. The Reverend Thomas Burns, born in Mauchline, Ayrshire, Scotland in 1796, was a nephew of Scotland's national bard Robert Burns. He was the spiritual leader of the pioneering Scots sailing from Greenock on the River Clyde on Saturday, 27th November 1847 onboard the ship, *Philip Laing*, arriving at Port Chalmers, Otago Harbour, South Island, New Zealand on Saturday 15th April. 1848.

On the 13th April they saw land, north east of Stewart Island, just before a remarkable sunset, and by the morning of the 14th they were off the mouth of the Clutha River at Molyneux Bay. On the Saturday morning, they reached Taioroa Head on the Otago Peninsula and it was here at 9.00am that the pilot Richard Driver came on board, taking charge of the ship, sailed it into Port Chalmers. Already at anchor in Otago Harbour was the John Wickcliffe, which had sailed from Gravesend on 24th September 1847. Violent storms had raged around the coast of Great Britain a few days after the ship's departure and the heavy-laden John Wickcliffe, the storeship for the expedition, sprang a leak in the English Channel, compelling her to shelter and refit in Portsmouth. Making fast after leaving Portsmouth she anchored off Port Chalmers on March 23rd 1848.

Deafening cheers were heard from both ships as the Phillip Laing's anchor plunged into the calm waters of the bay. By this time many of the passengers were on deck gazing at the surrounding steep wooded headlands of the harbour, many wondering how such a land could be cleared and ploughed. Burns whose practical agricultural knowledge explained that the rural lands lay behind the hills on the plains of the Clutha River, the Taieri and Tokomairiro and immediately anxiety gave way to happiness as the prospects of their new life seemed worth all the trials of their voyage.

The Rev Thomas Burns was regarded as a founder of Dunedin. Following the 1843 *Disruption* which had split the Church of Scotland, creating the new Free Church, the Rev Burns together with Captain William Cargill of Edinburgh, who had sailed on the John Wickcliffe, promoted the Free Church settlement in New Zealand. Thomas Burns personally selected the first migrants, many from Paisley near Glasgow, where the local weaving industry at the time was in recession. Keeping a pastoral eye on their welfare, whilst setting up a strong organisation for the Presbyterian Church in Otago. He supported public education and was the foundation chancellor of the University of Otago. Burns died in 1871, so the neo-Gothic Church of Otago, opened in 1873, the masterpiece of architect Robert Lawrence, became and remains a memorial to Thomas Burns's mission, as well as a striking Dunedin landmark. Burns resembled an Old Testament patriarch among the first settlers, a few condemning his stern puritanism, but he was well regarded by most of the settlers, as he was an energetic minister, who did everything expected of him. His farming skills, honed back on his father Gilbert Burns's farm in Ayrshire, gave him a love of the land and made him an ideal pioneer. His large funeral procession confirmed that these qualities were perhaps more appreciated following his death, than during his life.

Port Chalmers served as the port for the city of Dunedin. As the city grew with the increase in commerce following the Otago Gold Rush of the 1860s, and seeing over a three-month period 16,000 new arrivals pass through the Port, merchants pushed for the dredging of a channel. Named the Victoria Ship Channel, it was finally opened in 1881, along the north western side of Otago harbour allowing ocean going vessels to then reach the Port of Dunedin. Prior to this however, in the early 1870s construction began on the Port Chalmers Branch, a narrow-gauge railway link to Dunedin, subsequently being incorporated into the national rail network.

During the mid-1890s, the heroic era of Antarctic exploration, the Otago Harbour Board tried to attract explorers by extending generous hospitality, by way of coal, food and complimentary use of the harbour facilities. Famously, Robert Falcon Scott visited with both the *Discovery* in 1901 and his final doomed *Terra Nova* expedition in November 1910.

So it was, two years later, in the last days of December 1912, the Kalimpong migrants arrived at their destination, as the *Warrimoo* sailed into Dunedin dock. Six of the group disembarked and were met by their prospective employers. Two stayed on in Dunedin, the other four going to farms in the countryside around. Mary and David Ochterloney and the four others sailed on to Wellington, where two of the young men were dropped off, along with one of the girls, who was starting her nursing training. The three remaining were then ferried to Picton on South Island from Wellington, and it was here on South Island that Mary and Robert then continued by train to Blenheim. They were indemptured to a tobacco plantation owner in the Motueka, near Nelson area, providing work for locals and itinerant workers: topping plants, nipping out lateral shoots and picking leaves.

Captain James Cook, first sighting New Zealand in October 1769, made three further visits to the islands, by 1777. He and his crew using American tobacco as a standard trading tool. Eventually, production and manufacturing began in the early 20th century and the New Zealand Tobacco Company was established in 1913 in the Hawkes Bay region of North Island, ultimately becoming the National Tobacco Company in 1922.

Disembarking in Dunedin the six students were met by the Rev James S Ponder, the Honorary Secretary of the Settlement Committee, and Mrs W.L. Scott, Convenor of the Dunedin Ladies Committee. No great welcome this time - no tour of their new city, no speeches and no civic celebratory tea. Instead, the young friends, Dolly included, were immediately forwarded to their host families and on to their respective destinations. The boys to farms and the two girls to domestic service. No last-minute goodbyes, no hugs, no well-wishing and after weeks of leisurely days at sea pondering their futures, the final farewell was over in minutes. Although the group had grown up together, laughed together, cried together at times, in the last six weeks or so their friendships had deepened. Separated in early childhood from their parents, growing up in a strict presbyterian environment, the children turned to each other for support, and close bonds were formed. The bonds shared were that of colour, backgrounds of mixed parentage and illegitimacy. Like greenhouse plants in a protected atmosphere, the group were now far from their shielded environment. Alone to face the truth of the real world, a changing world furthermore, as World War One was only some 20 months away. Sadly, these young men and women would never be a group again.

Alone now in a new and very different country, Dolly, aged twenty, was placed with a Dunedin family as a domestic help. Apart from cleaning, washing and ironing, she found herself doing food shopping and having to deal with money, something not only foreign to her, but also a foreign currency. However, unlike most of her Kalimpong friends and companions, she blended in with the family and surroundings, so in the close community she now found herself, Dolly did not stand out, looking more like a *home girl*. The hours were long, with only one afternoon off a week, and she also had to attend church with the family on a Sunday. So, in many ways things weren't so different from the Homes, just a new sort isolation and seclusion in a very different part of the world.

The years of cheerful companionship, friendship and close understandings, were over.

CHAPTER 43
Dunedin, New Zealand
1913-1915

Fortunately Dolly fitted into the household, enjoying her trips into town to do the shopping, and mastering all her tasks to the family's satisfaction. Sundays were her favourite time, morning service with the family, after which she was free to go out and make her acquaintance with Dunedin. One of her favourite places was the Dunedin Botanic Gardens established in 1863, and the oldest botanical garden in New Zealand. After extensive flooding in 1868 the gardens were moved to their current site the following year, forming a green belt around the inner part of the city. There were several pathways around the gardens, with seating arranged to allow visitors to enjoy the best views, or to peacefully appreciate the various plant collections artfully displayed. Especially spectacular were the long herbaceous borders and the five coloured borders at the north end of the lower gardens, always greatly admired and enjoyed by all.

Dolly arrived in Dunedin in mid-summer when the rose garden was at its most colourful. She loved spending time there among the beds and borders of select species roses, of old garden roses and of the many varieties she had not seen before. Dolly so enjoyed their exciting colours but especially their sweet scent. The Winter Garden glasshouse had only been built in 1908 with many plants from warmer, humid environments; palms, tropical trees and shrubs which would not survive outside in Dunedin's cool temperate climate. Dolly enjoyed the Winter Garden, where sitting in the warmth reminded her of her family home and garden in Calcutta. It was here one afternoon, whilst sitting enjoying the plants and her memories, Dolly became aware of someone watching her, before coming forward and speaking to her. She lifted her head, and found herself looking into the soft brown eyes of a handsome, dark haired young man, perhaps a little older than herself. He smiled and said, 'Kia ora', mentioning he had seen her sitting here before, and wondered if she came from Dunedin or was just visiting. Replying, Dolly said she lived and worked in Dunedin, but was not from Dunedin, and yes, she came most Sunday afternoons. The young man introduced himself as Lex Thorpe and asked her if she would like to walk round the gardens with him and he would show her the native New Zealand plant displays. The colourful grasses and tussocks grown throughout the gardens, provided colourful contrasts to the green ferns and southern beech trees. Most were new to Dolly of course, and she asked many questions. Wandering on, forgetting the time, the couple were not only engrossed in their conversation but their surroundings.

Suddenly distracted and realising the time, Dolly knew she would need to get back before dinnertime or the family would be wondering where she was, if not already.
Thanking Lex for his interesting and friendly company, she said she would have to go and catch the bus back to her place of work in the suburb of Roslyn, which was also her home now, as she was a live-in domestic servant. Lex understood and walked her out of the gardens and back to the bus stop, waiting with her till the bus arrived. He said that he had enjoyed his afternoon too and hoped they might meet up again another Sunday, and he would be looking forward to that. 'Haera ra' was Lex's goodbye.

As Dolly stepped onto the bus saying she would look out for him, she felt her feelings lift, and smiling to herself, she looked out of the bus window hoping to catch a glimpse of Lex as he crossed the road. Hoping she would not be too late by the time she made it back after her lovely escapade, she sat back and pondered her afternoon's meeting. The family having had visitors all afternoon, and enjoying tea and soft drinks in the garden, were only saying goodbye to their friends when Dolly arrived home. Making her way into the house and up to her room, she freshened up, changing back into her simple uniform before heading down to the kitchen, to start preparing the evening meal of cold cuts and salad, followed by fresh kiwi fruit and ice cream. Dolly's mind kept drifting back to the warm afternoon and her new friend, hoping they would meet up sometime soon again. These new feelings and imaginings kept her warm throughout the next couple of weeks till she managed her next visit to the Botanic Gardens.

Dolly asked her employer, Mrs McMillan, if she would find out where her friend from Kalimpong, Mary Ochterlony was living and working, as she would like to write to her to keep in touch, nowS they were both settled into their new lives. This Mrs McMillan did and soon Dolly and Mary were exchanging personal secrets and the old friendship being rekindled, lasted many years.

CHAPTER 44
Dunedin to Christchurch
1916 – 1918

Signing up in their thousands, young men hopeful of becoming soldiers, fought and died at Gallipoli, Palestine and the Western Front in France and Belgium. Around 12,000 died in or because of the war, with the remains of thousands sadly left far from home. Of the 10,000 New Zealand horses sent to the Front, only four returned.

Lex Thorpe, one of over 2,000 Māori who served with New Zealand forces, signed up late summer 1916. With mounting casualties and the need for reinforcements on the Gallipoli Peninsula it forced a change in imperial policy regarding *native peoples* fighting. Māori had mixed views about the war, some supporting and rushing to sign up, with others opposing as they did not want to fight for the British Crown which had been seen to have done much harm to the Māori communities in the 19th century.

Leaving New Zealand's shores for winter in war torn Europe, Lex was one of the 12,000 countrymen who died on the Western Front, and one of 360 Māori killed due to the conflict.

Leaving behind a bewildered Dolly on the Dunedin station platform, where for many, it would be the last time they would see their loved ones. Now alone in early pregnancy, and having to face her employers with the certainty of losing not only her employment, but her home. Wondering where could she go, what could she do, as the world seemed to have far greater worries at this time than a young, pregnant immigrant also far from home, the only home she had ever really known.

Writing again to Mary telling her what had happened and asking if she had any ideas who she should contact and where should she go? Mary immediately replied, concerned about her friend, suggesting she should get in touch with The Homes at Kalimpong and ask for help and advice. Dr Graham in his wisdom would be able to suggest a solution she was sure, and perhaps even offer some kind of help, he knew so many people around the world. Waiting patiently every day hoping to hear something from 'Daddy Graham', till she realised she could no longer put off telling Mrs McMillan about her predicament.

Dolly never did receive a reply from the Homes or Dr Graham.

There was disappointment, of course, as the McMillan family had grown fond of Dolly and had hoped she would marry, settle down in Dunedin, and continue working for them. This was not to be. Unmarried and bearing a child was not acceptable, certainly not in the strict Free Church community. The city of Christchurch would be better they suggested, and so it was that Dolly headed off to Christchurch for the first time, her ticket paid for, and to an address arranged for by her employers.

Standing alone among the other passengers, on the mosaic tiled platform of the grandest of all railway stations, completed in 1906, George Troup's stunning Dunedin station, with soaring towers and stained-glass windows, where she had said goodbye to Lex, became Dolly's final, poignant memory of Dunedin. The frieze of cherubs beneath the balcony gazed down on Dolly as she wondered what her next journey would bring. Having had great hopes when she first stepped off the *Warrimoo* at Dunedin harbour four years earlier, and seeming a long time ago, she still missed her childhood friends from Kalimpong. Where would they be? The boys away to war perhaps, she thought unhappily, with only Mary keeping in touch.

-oOo-

The Christchurch Female Home had opened in the 1870s as a rescue home for unmarried pregnant women. The home had been established by religious and charitable organisations, with women admitted during pregnancy and giving birth there. The girls before and after the births did domestic work in the homes, intended to keep them focused on homely and motherly duties, hopefully enabling them to be more employable later, when moving on, mostly without their babies. Only a few of the young women like Dolly kept their babies, caring for them in the nursery.

Her daughter, Kathleen, was born on Saturday 25th April 1917. She was an attractive baby, with dark wavy hair and lovely brown eyes like her late father Lex. Dolly stayed on in the Home helping with the daily domestic duties. Her experience in the Lucia King Cottage in Kalimpong with the youngest children and babies, gave her the confidence to be a great help here in Christchurch.

One morning unexpectedly Dolly was called to the Matron's office and advised that they had managed to find her domestic employment with a lady in the city, where she would have a room for herself and Kathleen, and a small wage as her accommodation and food would be included. Although realising she could not stay in the Home forever, she felt sad when she finally had to move on once more, this time to live with the Ensor family in central Christchurch.

The year was now 1918.

CHAPTER 45
Christchurch
The 1918 Pandemic – Spanish Flu

Between October and December 1918, the Influenza Pandemic cost New Zealand half as many lives, as it had lost in the course of the Great War. No other occurrence had killed so many New Zealanders in such a short space of time. The pandemic was easing however by the time Dolly moved into the city centre in mid-summer. Nevertheless, the national death toll was thought to have been around 9,000, with more men than women dying, whereas in most other countries affected by the pandemic more women than men died.

No one was sure how the pandemic arose, many believing, though this was disproved, that it was borne by a deadly new virus that had arrived a couple of months earlier on the Royal Mail liner *Niagara* sailing out of America on 12th October. Māori suffered heavily, losing over 2,000 people. Deaths did not occur evenly among Māori and Pakeha, white New Zealanders. Some areas were badly hit, whilst others escaped largely unscathed. The only places struck with unvarying severity were military camps, and it was from military camps in the American States of Kansas, Georgia and South Carolina that the virus had originally spread, first to Europe and later to the southern hemisphere. Most public facilities and businesses were closed, and public events and gatherings cancelled. The medical workforce, already stretched due to the war, was augmented by volunteers working in their local community. As always, the public sought answers from government, which in due course passed the 1920 Health Act, a beneficial legacy of the pandemic.

The Ensor family lived in Dean Street, Christchurch, overlooking Hagley Park.
Their business having volunteered contributions toward the upkeep of the Christchurch Female Home, the Matron decided to contact Mrs Ensor, a widow, with three sons serving in the war, to see if she would employ Dolly as a lady's help or domestic servant. Two of her sons were then missing in action on the Western Front, presumed dead, the third returning home, injured though not seriously, was soon able to take up the senior position in the family business, taking over from his late father. Mrs Ensor agreed to employ Dolly, who fitted in well to life in the Ensor household. She worked hard helping in any way she could, especially cleaning, keeping them all as safe as possible from the influenza. She was lucky too, being able to walk out in the cool fresh autumnal air around the park opposite their home, pushing Kathleen in a well-used pram, handed in by a friend of the family. Dolly also enjoyed walking into town to do shopping for Mrs Ensor, and bringing back fresh ingredients for their cook who worked Monday to Friday. Dolly making light meals at the weekend, was soon increasing her abilities in the kitchen, watched by a contented Kathleen sitting in her highchair.

The War ended, the pandemic ended, and eventually life slowly returned to normal. In 1920, Edward, Prince of Wales, King George V's eldest son, visited New Zealand, mainly to thank the Dominion for its contribution to the Empire's war effort. He arrived in April and spent four weeks travelling the country aboard a lavishly appointed train and motor coach. Journeys that Dolly too would travel in years to come, but not with such luxury. Mobbed by adoring crowds wherever he went, though he was seemingly less impressed, complaining in letters home to his mistress of the day, *of never having a free hour away from returned soldiers or cheering school children.*
His worst insults were for the Governor-General, Lord Liverpool,

who it seemed to him was *pricelessly pompous*. Lord Liverpool, Arthur William de Brito Savile Foljambe was born in Eastbourne, England. He fought in the Boer War, was the 2nd Earl of Liverpool, and New Zealand's first Governor-General. Originally appointed the 18th Governor of New Zealand in 1912, previously having been Comptroller of the Royal Household. The office was raised to Governor-General and his term extended to 1920. His father, the first Earl, had served in the Naval Brigade in New Zealand in the 1860s.

Managing to persuade Mrs Ensor to allow them a couple of hours off, Dolly and the cook, Jeanette, made their way into Cathedral Square pushing Kathleen in her pram, joining the jostling throng, and hoping to catch a glimpse of the Royal Prince. Returning to Dean Street smiling and chattering away, eager to report to Mrs Ensor who seemed less impressed, as both young women it seemed were more carried away with the exciting atmosphere, as when asked about the prince, they both said they only saw his hat.

Also in 1920, New Zealand sent its first team to the Summer Olympics, held in Antwerp, Belgium. Although having had to endure nine weeks of travel, the team of five performed well, returning with a bronze medal. Another well-known figure visited in 1920, Arthur Conan Doyle, the author of the Sherlock Holmes detective stories. Touring New Zealand lecturing on Christian Spiritualism, he hoped the tour would help foster a surge in its popularity. As his claims of scientific proof were flimsy, he was ridiculed in newspapers, which sought to expose him as a fraud and charlatan. This time Mrs Ensor did not give permission for Dolly and Jeanette to go to one of his well-publicised lectures, as she thought it most foolish, putting more silly ideas into their young heads, already filling with the new innovations of radio, cinema, gramophones and motor cars that marked the beginning of the roaring twenties. It was at this time, that Dolly became aware that her boss's son was showing inappropriate interest in her at every opportunity. This was not unusual, and in the spring of 1920 with more threats of unemployment and homelessness, Dolly was raped repeatedly by him. Finding herself pregnant again, the result of course was the same, but sadder this time, as Dolly had to come to the heart-breaking decision of having her lovely daughter Kathleen, soon to be four, adopted.

CHAPTER 46
Christchurch to Nelson
1921-1923

Douglas, Dolly's second child, was born approaching winter on Saturday 21St May 1921. A strong, healthy boy with rosy cheeks and strawberry blond hair, quite different colouring from Kathleen. Realising that Douglas could be her grandson, but never saying, Mrs Ensor suggested after much enquiry, a childless couple of comfortable means, as prospective adoptive parents for Kathleen. Difficult as this was for Dolly, she realised that Kathleen would have a better life with this caring couple, who could certainly comfortably provide for her, more than she ever could. Especially now with a new baby, no job and little money.

Mrs Ensor allowed Dolly to stay till she found another position, this time answering an advert in the *Nelson Evening Mail*. So, with a sad heart she said goodbye to Mrs Ensor, who had always been kind to her, and her friend Jeanette. With her new baby and what little luggage she had, Dolly set off on her next journey, by bus this time, to Nelson. Departing from outside the Bus Exchange on Lichfield Street in Christchurch, for the seven-and-a-half-hour journey the bus followed the spectacular rugged Kaikoura coastline. On north to Blenheim, where she remembered her friends Margaret and Robert Ochterloney had been sent to work on a tobacco farm back in early 1913. Then crossing the Richmond Range to Havelock and down to Wakapuaka, the bus eventually arrived in Nelson, nestling at the head of Tasman Bay. There were fortunately a few stops along the way, as travelling with a young baby was not easy.

The two parallel Kaikoura Ranges located in the northeast of South Island two hours north of Christchurch was where the bus stopped first, at the coastal village of Kaikoura. It lay between the native bush clad Seaward Kaikoura Range reaching down to the coast and usually snow-capped in winter, and the windblown seascapes, where seals, and playful dolphins could be seen leaping out of the water, and further out to sea, whales blowing. After enjoying the short break in the fresh air, and a welcome cup of tea at the local shop along with several of the other passengers, Dolly was soon back on the bus. She settled down into her seat again, and after giving Doug some of his bottle soon both mother and baby were asleep, as the bus continued on its way to Nelson.

Thankfully Douglas was quite content to lie in his mother's arms gazing around him, never crying. Arriving in Nelson at the main bus stance on Bridge Street, in the early evening and already dark, Dolly and the baby were met by a taxi arranged by Mrs Ensor for which she was so grateful. She had also given Dolly an envelope with money to help her get started in her new position, but more importantly to help with baby Doug.

Dolly arrived at 5 Wellington Street, Nelson, a white clapboard house with a well-ordered and colourful garden. Her new employer, an elderly man who had spent most of his life on fishing boats, now enjoyed gardening since his retiral. Still owning a couple of fishing boats which he rented out, giving him extra income, which allowed him to employ Dolly as a housekeeper and cook.

She soon settled in to the daily routine, and though a bachelor all his days, Max Webby really enjoyed having a baby in the house and was charmed watching Douglas grow, day by day. A happy, contented child, who loved Max's fun and attention. Soon Dolly knew her way around Nelson. The local people, a mixture of Maori and Pakeha were friendly, stopping to speak to the baby and have a few words with Dolly when she was out shopping. Max had acquired an old pram from a neighbour, and enjoyed cleaning and polishing it up for Douglas. Friends also knitted blankets and baby clothes, and propped up against his pillows Doug watched all that was going on around him, and enjoyed the admiration of passers-by. His mother loved Doug, especially his big smile which somehow helped deaden the pain of losing Kathleen. Always wondering how and where she was, and if she remembered her, it haunted her and was never far from her mind. Yet still finding she could never speak about her to anyone.

Dolly having settled into her new life and routine, sent her new Nelson address to Mary, letting her know how things were, and asking if she had ever heard from others in the Kennedy Group. Perhaps even from Dr Graham. Guessing there would have been big changes in Kalimpong – perhaps even new cottages, new house parents, and of course new children, with few now remembering the 'Kennedy Batch'. It was ten years since they left India, yet somehow Kalimpong, Darjeeling and Calcutta, though far away, in her mind, still felt like home.

CHAPTER 47
Nelson to Coal Creek Flats
1923-1925

Dolly, now in her early thirties, still unmarried and with a young son, found her work and son taking up most of her time. Max however, encouraged her to spend time in the garden, which she really enjoyed. The climate was ideal for roses and vegetables. Under his watchful eye and guidance, she spent many happy hours tending the plants. Feeling more peaceful here than she had felt for a long time. The fruits of her labours, were enjoyed not only at the dinner table, but throughout the house, with many vases of colourful roses. The garden brought back memories of the highly competitive annual cottage garden competitions, at Dr Graham's in Kalimpong. Memories too of the gardens in Rangoon, Penang and even Dunedin where she first met Lex, Kathleen's father, one of thousands who never returned home from the Great War, maybe even lying in an unmarked grave.

During her years in New Zealand, Dolly never spoke about her childhood in India. No need really, being Caucasian, so more a 'home girl' in looks. She had managed to slip through the net of racism which, had affected many of the Kalimpong settlers and her time in Nelson was no different. Max had treated her and Doug like the family he never had, and often baby-sat of an evening to let Dolly spend time in one of the many cafes in the main square, chatting and enjoying the company of other people around her own age.

Standing on the eastern shores of the Bay of Tasman, and named after the British admiral, Horatio Nelson, it was South Island's oldest city. Renowned for its natural landscapes, long golden beaches, untouched forests, mountains, and lovely weather. It always attracted creative people, artists, musicians and writers, and it was here one evening that Dolly met a younger man, who was interested in music and choirs and they got talking over a coffee. Not realising how quickly the evening had gone in, Dolly hurriedly excused herself. As the group waved goodbye, the tall, dark-haired, good-looking young man rose, offering to walk her home. She accepted. Arriving at Max's house, Colin, who had introduced himself by this time said he would like to meet her again, smiling, Dolly agreed. Their friendship grew and Dolly looked forward to her weekly evening off. Eventually she explained about Doug, and soon on her monthly Sunday afternoons off, the trio headed out in Colin's car to explore the surrounding area.

The Brook Sanctuary, only four miles from Nelson, became their favourite haunt. Having no natural predators, native birds thrived, filling the trees with birdsong as the trio explored the nature trails. Dolly loved it, and Doug high on Colin's shoulders, squealed with delight. They spent many happy hours enjoying this natural nature reserve. They also went to Tahunanui Beach with its shallow, calm waters, ideal for playing in and swimming. Young Doug thrived in these happy natural surroundings, as did Dolly.

Doug was two years old in May 1923 when Dolly realised, she was pregnant again. Max too had noticed that Dolly was pregnant, advising her to contact Colin. Becoming distant, their outings ceased, leaving Dolly bewildered, especially when learning that Colin was already married and his wife was pregnant and their son was born in September. A few months later in January 1924 Hector was born. Within a day or two of the birth, Colin sent word that if she was agreeable, he would put an advertisement in the local paper the *Nelson Evening Mail*, - kind lady wanted to adopt baby *boy.* Dolly agreed. In fact, it was Colin's 53-year-old mother Ethel who answered the advertisement. She and her husband James would be delighted to adopt the baby boy, their farm at Golden Bay being an ideal place for the boy to grow up. So, Hector Higgins became Hector Crichton. Young Doug was with Dolly the day she handed Hector over to his new mother at the front gate of Max's house. Doug was crying, not fully understanding as he clung to Dolly's dress, hiding from the white-haired, but kind faced lady.

Dolly stayed on in Wellington Road for some time, Max, having no wish to see them go, allowing Dolly time to recover from the birth and the separation from the baby. She and Doug both flourished in the peaceful environment. Eventually time came to move away from the Nelson area, having seen Colin several times in town with his wife and baby son, Dolly knew in her heart it was not an ideal situation. Searching the papers once more, she found an advert for a *housekeeper - help* at Coal Creek Flats on the West Coast. Dolly replied to Sidney Stuart's advert and soon after, hearing she had been accepted for the post, with a heavy heart she and young Doug said a tearful farewell to Max, setting off for Greymouth on the train from Christchurch.

Sidney Stewart, a dairy farmer, was around twenty-five years older than Dolly. He was a widower, his wife Catherine Rose having died in childbirth many years ago, their baby daughter, Virginia Rose, a few days later. He met Dolly, and a very tired Doug off the train at Still Water Junction. With only a few belongings in a couple of bags, Sidney helped mother and son up onto the horse drawn wagon. In silence they made their way along the road to Coal Creek. This would be Dolly's home for the next fourteen years. Doug's for less.

CHAPTER 48

1912
The End of a Long Voyage
and
a
Hopeful New Beginning

The Rev James S. Ponder, the Church Session and Mrs W.L. Scott, convenor of the Dunedin Ladies Committee, had received word from their friend Dr John Graham of Kalimpong, that a group of Homes Students would soon be boarding the SS *Sangola* at Calcutta, and sailing on to Melbourne, via Rangoon and Penang. After a few days visiting Melbourne, the group would board the SS *Warimoo* for Dunedin. Dr Graham's second communication, wished them well on their arrival in Dunedin, their next destination and new home. He also related the press report of the following day after the rousing send off in Calcutta and of how proud he was of Miss Kennedy's group. The message unfortunately arrived a few days after the group had landed, but was none the less welcome by Rev Ponder and his congregation. Prior to the students' arrival there had been many meetings of the various church groups, and contact with local people, as the church was seeking suitable employment and of course accommodation for the young migrants. Many members of the congregation came forward, keen to offer their support, and by the time the young group landed, plans though rushed, were finally in place.

Unlike the three other welcoming committees, The Ladies Committee of Dunedin decided there was no great need for a welcoming extravaganza. Feeling it more appropriate if the arrival was kept simple, with no long goodbyes, just an unassuming meeting on the dockside, matching the chosen families with the students. The Rev Ponder agreed, feeling that getting the young people settled right away was the best plan – perhaps a small get together could be arranged for later.

As the *Warimoo* eased its way into its berth, with horns blowing, ropes being flung over onto the quayside to waiting dockers, and with lots of shouting and waving from passengers to waiting families and friends, all adding to general buzz of excitement. Many of the passengers were pleased to be returning home to New Zealand from Australia and further afield, including the Kalimpong group's chaperone Miss Mary Kennedy after several years as a house parent.

Dolly, dressed again in her long white frock and sun hat; with her long dark pleat falling over her shoulder she approached the gangway. She held her bags close to her, especially the smallest bag containing the little silver rattle her mother had given her all those years ago in Calcutta. There was elbowing and jostling as passengers excitedly pushed their way forward. It was then Dolly lost sight of Mary and her brother Robert, but with the other passengers eager to disembark, Dolly was moved along quicker than she would have wished. Mary and her brother Robert were remaining onboard as they were sailing on to Wellington, and Dolly had wanted to say a last fond goodbye. It was not to be. Carefully, but with some trepidation, Dolly stepped up on to the gangway, holding her breath as she gazed down on all the upturned faces, wondering who would be meeting her. Fleetingly she remembered the noise, smell, heat and hubbub of Calcutta dock, wondering if this was how her Aunt Dorothea must have felt, all those years ago.

'Oh God, our Father, what is in front of me, what will happen to me? Please keep me safe.' Dolly prayed under her breath, edging her way slowly down the gangway, before eventually stepping on to New Zealand soil for the first time to an unknown future.

> The End
> and
> The Beginning.

Printed in Great Britain
by Amazon